Z-

BY EDWIN GILBERT

Native Stone
The Squirrel Cage
Silver Spoon
The Hourglass
Jamie
The Beautiful Life
American Chrome

A Season in

Monte Carlo A NOVEL BY

EDWIN GILBERT

ARBOR HOUSE
NEW YORK

Library of Congress Catalogue Card Number: 75–40512

ISBN: 0–87795–131–4

Manufactured in the United States of America

Second Printing, 1976

FOR INGRID

AUTHOR'S NOTE *Since this is a novel occasional liberties with facts are permitted and have been taken. And though some actual places or people are mentioned by name this is merely because they contribute to the authentic ambiance of Monte Carlo, and in no way bear any relation to any of the fictional characters or incidents of this narrative.*

E.G.

PART I *June*

When it was all over I could look back and put it together with more clarity and perspective. While much of it was going on I happened to be in Monte Carlo working on a project, and I had occasion to meet a number of other Americans who lived there. Many of them were extremely rich, though not all. Among them were the three figures who were to become central to this work: Nick, Sheldon, John.

Of course there was no way of knowing or accepting the circumstance that unnatural death would be touching any of the group: for one thing, the Monte Carlo police, with their penchant for dossiers, are regarded as among the toughest and most assiduous in the world.

In point of fact, there is little crime in Monte Carlo. Muggings are rare, rape and murder virtually unknown. For the most part when the law is broken it is in a rather old-fashioned, even genteel way: the theft of jewels or works of art.

Yet ironically the biggest arms traders in the world—Zaharoff, Cummings and, more recently, the upstart munitions manipulator John McFarland — have made Monte Carlo their home base.

Nevertheless all remains peace and law and order.

Maybe that's why none of us was prepared for any sort of criminality or violence.

At any rate, I became preoccupied with this community, which, true or false, is said to be one of the most opulent tax shelters in the world. And certain aspects caught my surprise:

For example, none of these men (nor the women) was afflicted by the gambler's virus except perhaps Nick, who occasionally used slot machines as instruments of superstition; none ran to the Casino or the gaming tables; none was drawn here by the clichés and myths Monte Carlo had spawned around the globe.

Also, like most people, I'd assumed that rich Americans merely had to skip off to certain spots outside the United States and their tax problems would be over. Later I was not so sure. For other problems became superimposed. The tax haven, I saw, was indeed a silken escape hatch but in Monte Carlo I began to recognize what it could do to those who used or abused it, and the way emotions could become magnified when one lives in such hothouse isolation . . .

Anyway, it was here on this rocky promontory of the Riviera that the lives of these three Americans became linked: later I would view it as forming a kind of somber triptych painted by fate or karma, the colors earthy, compounded by human greed, need, self-deceit and love; by the urge to flee the terrors lurking on the nocturnal streets of Los Angeles or Miami or New York; or by the hope for respite from life-long frustrations or the hope for a second chance to regain something one had lost.

Yet none of them ever realized that what he was running away from or what he was running toward might elude him — surely, each must have believed that there was no better or wiser way to fulfill life than here in this gilded and protective principality so far from the homeland.

For all this there has to be a beginning, and what I recall is how, at first, much of it seemed so sunny, not at all grave, almost comedic, giving little portent of what was to come. Beginnings seldom do.

I

To begin: Harper Nicholson (Nick) was born in New York, 1940. Public primary school; prepped at Kent on a scholarship, attended Brown University, dropped out. The Philadelphia Main Line fortune his family had inherited had been lost in the great stock debacle, so that Nick grew up in a household lean on money and fat on gentility. In 1960 his widowed father got him a job with a Wall Street brokerage house but Nick was dismissed when he told one of the firm's major clients that the company's executive vice-president (listed in the *Social Register*) was a crook in the pay of a Texas oil company . . .

Nick's next stellar performance came when he took a position in the administrative offices of a New York hospital: after six months in this debasing ambience, he was ushered out for distributing Hershey bars

16

among the diabetic patients, becoming in their eyes, however briefly, a saint . . .

When the fetid breath of the Vietnam war came too close, he accepted a new scholarship, this one at the Sorbonne in Paris. He quit after a while and bummed around the Continent with another dude, Hy Greenspan, an anti-war buddy who, like Nick, was wanted by the FBI for being a "coward."

When funds ran out, Nick took up with a woman of a certain age. This was a mistake. For instead of needed cash she kept giving him cashmere sweaters. Though several ladies made overtures, Nick decided to go straight and became a tour guide for a large American travel company, ending up doing the Monte Carlo beat.

From this job he was harshly expelled. Even now, ten years later in 1975, he talks about it once in a while:

Look, it was just that I finally got so nauseated by my spiel about the Monte Carlo Casino, Gracious Princess Grace, Aristotle Onassis, his yacht *Christina,* the Oceanographic Museum, the Grand Prix race, and all the jazz about gamblers, suicides, and the glamorous jet-set cats who reside there—the whole *shmear,* as Hy Greenspan would say—that I suddenly snatched up the microphone in my sweaty fingers one sweltering August afternoon at the end of the ride and addressed my bus load of American passengers, laying it down something like this:

"Well, folks, now you've seen Monaco and I've

told you everything I'm supposed to. I did omit
mentioning the fact that it's something of a tax shelter. Sounds crafty or cunning? Maybe it is. But that's
not the point. If there's any point at all it's that
maybe tax shelters might be the last gasp or death
rattle of our great System. Didn't someone once say
that in life only two things are inevitable: death and
taxes? Well, you can't escape death but if you're rich,
real rich, and live here, you can avoid a hell of a lot
of taxes. In Monaco you don't have to pay them a
nickel on your earnings, and you don't have to pay a
capital gains tax either, nor a death tax. And one more
thing, folks, Uncle Sam can't get a hold of you here,
tax evasion is not a criminal offense over here and so
you can't be extradited. It's right here in Monte Carlo
where certain big wheels are said to legally ream the
Internal Revenue Service and hide their operations.
In fact, come to think of it, almost every foreign
resident here is hiding out from something. Or someone. Or himself, maybe. And don't they say everybody who hides out or hides in dies a little every day
along the way . . . ?

"What's that, sir? If I feel that way why do I keep
sticking around? I'll tell you a secret: I'm not. As of
now I'm going to cut out. Head back to the Big
Apple."

Back in New York Nick's centerfold good looks
catapulted him into modeling, TV commercials,
promoting whiskey, cars and other macho products.
From this he graduated to a new life style, one rather

high off the hog and special: he became a walking jewelry case for an international firm as prestigious as Cartier's or Van Cleef & Arpels, while also working as a walking clotheshorse for an organization not unlike Cardin or Yves St. Laurent. Major social events at major social watering holes found Nick among those present. By then he had teamed up with Simona, who was his female counterpart, and they sold everything off their bodies—selling, stripping, happily screwing their way from New York to Palm Beach, to Barbados to Sardinia. In Sardinia their affair ended, as did their jobs. Simona hitched a cruise to Monte Carlo and Nick made it back to New York.

In New York this is what happened to him: he met Jane. He married her because she was a wonderful girl and because he had got her pregnant. Less than four months afterward she was dead. A single night, the one night Nick was away from their apartment in the old brownstone on East 88th Street. That night it had happened, the same sort of banal incident he read about in the newspapers every day. Except it had happened to Jane: the fire escape break-in, the hostile, sick thief needing money, and Jane screaming so hysterically that the man silenced her. Strangling out the last cry. This too he saw reported in the papers, a brief paragraph concluding with the information that the man had been "released a month ago from Bellevue where he had been under psychiatric observation."

When Nick left New York this time it was for the last time.

Simona had written him stating that she knew of an ideal way for him to make a living if he wanted to leave America.

At that moment there was nothing he wanted more.

Within a few years Nick had become an integral part of the very milieu he had once so facetiously criticized. Except that now it was different. Now he felt differently. His eyes saw differently:

Now he had a purpose, a new direction . . .

Anyway Harper Nicholson, at age thirty-five, was a sort of hustler. But of a very special kind, which is to say he was more interested in opportunities than opportunism.

He was into real estate in Monte Carlo. And whatever ancillary or unexpected bonuses might fall his way.

Nick was among the twenty-five thousand Americans and other foreigners who were residents (legally or otherwise) of Monaco, a whopping majority as opposed to the native Monégasques, about five thousand souls whose disinterest in gambling is only countered by their pride in the Monaco soccer team. Most of the local people function within the Monte Carlo sector, a very small sector indeed, since all of

Monaco is only about 500 acres, or half the size of New York's Central Park. It might be easy to laugh at this mini-principality except that unemployment is non-existent, and there is no income tax; the budget balances and the annual revenue in 1974 was more than seventy-five million dollars. Prince Rainier, the last absolute monarch in the Western world, runs the whole show (he can invite anyone to become a citizen or he can expel anyone from his state) but he runs it less like a prince than a corporation executive, and not without the considerable asset of his Philadelphia wife.

Centuries before the invasion of today's tourists, the Phoenicians invaded this strategic and sun-blessed area; and they in turn were followed by the Greeks and the Romans. In 1297 Monaco was seized by François Grimaldi and in 1529 it fell to Spain. But by 1860 the Grimaldis had recovered their sovereignty and by 1911 the first constitution was enacted into law.

The musical comedy image of Monte Carlo has been somewhat marred by such unfrivolous activities as the reclamation of more than fifty acres of land along the seacoast, as well as the creation of a complex of light industry which produces a wide spectrum of sophisticated items from electric razors to electronic devices for the Concorde SST jetliner and the myriad components of household appliances.

But who can quibble? Prosperity abounds in this postage stamp of a country which has spawned twenty-nine banks, forty-five real estate agencies, almost two hundred construction companies and more than two thousand businesses.

If that is not impressive, there is another fact: Monaco is one of the last urban communities in the world where a woman can go out after dark without fear of being molested.

Prince Rainier III and his government company, the Société des Bains de Mer (S.B.M.), are very sensitive to the caprices of tourism, for Monte Carlo has twice been struck poor. Two world wars, world depressions and other upheavals have taken their tolls of tourism. The Prince, determined to rejuvenate the moribund condition of Monaco after World War II, had to buck his old friend Aristotle Onassis to regain the controlling interest in S.B.M., which happens to own the Casino, the Hotel de Paris, the Hotel Hermitage, the Summer Sporting Club, and other flourishing institutions.

In the corporate manner, United States market analysts were engaged to make studies in depth of Monaco's tourist potential, and French computer experts probed the Casino's operations: the economic health of this mini-principality, circa 1975, can be said to be robust and secure.

Monte Carlo, it ought to be noted, is not Monaco and Monaco is not Monte Carlo. The principality is divided into three districts:

At the western end is the Rock on which the palace of the Grimaldis and the 13th century city are found, as well as the Oceanographic Museum presided over by renowned undersea explorer Jacques Cousteau. Below the museum, set in the great crag of seacoast wall, is the old jail: the occasional inmates enjoy the same picturesque vistas as any guest in the royal suite of the Hotel de Paris.

The lower or center city, La Condamine, houses all the civil services of the principality, features an arcaded open air market and a tangle of traffic.

Eastward, beyond the harbor, is Monte Carlo, the modern shopping area, the bailiwick of such non-discount houses as Cartier, Lanvin, Pucci, Hermès, etc. It is the homeground of the Casino and the Hotel de Paris. This five-star hostelry has housed in its elegant accommodations during the past hundred years a gallery of personalities from the Dowager Queen of Russia, Pierpont Morgan, the Aga Khan, William K. Vanderbilt to Winston Churchill (as well as, during the Nazi occupation, the Gestapo).

Since Monaco is wedged between sea and mountain, land is at a premium: old villas have been demolished and given way to towering condominiums so that the apartments rising in tiers suggest the future shock of a principality of prisms.

On another level it ought to be said that the school system and the hospital and medical facilities are more than adequate; and that among the dentists there is an American one, while among the butchers there is a kosher one.

Even the climate defines the life style. The sun shines for most of the year, sunlight indiscriminately touching the baroque domes of the Casino, the terraces of the Hotel de Paris, the chrome grilles of the innumerable Rolls-Royces or the office windows of the secret police from whom even the most artful of dodgers can't always hide:

One of the most artful ways to hide in Monte Carlo is *not* to hide — that is, merge with the mob who shows up in the barroom of the superchic Hotel de Paris, a chip's throw from the Casino . . .

This room was, in effect, Nick's office; the bar was his desk.

But Nick sometimes viewed it as an aquarium, all the specimens, catalogued or not, visible and some of them even worth watching.

This particular night the pickings, even for an ignorant ichthyologist, were not too bad. In fact, most any evening here, a brand-name angler might hook the Count of Barcelona, father of the heir to the new Spanish monarchy; or catch the blue-jeaned species whose father happens to be Stavros Niarchos. Coming up for air from time to time might be, in alphabetical order: Baldwin (Billy or Jimmy), Caine (Michael), Ford (Christina or Henry), Lasker (Mary), Khan (the Aga or Begum), Niven (David), Nureyev (Rudolph), Peck (Gregory), Rothschild (Baron E. de), Shaw (Irwin), Taylor (Liz), Thyssen (Baron Heini). . .

But right now it was the ones at that corner table who held Nick's attention: the arms trader, John McFarland and his wife Marie with Sheldon Bradley. And it was Bradley who was the goldfish Nick hoped to net and maneuver into a condo, a transaction that would bring into Nick's impoverished coffers at least five percent commission (tax free and no overhead) on an apartment sale of about half a million dollars.

What counted was that if he netted Sheldon Bradley, he would be able to slay all the dragons of his debts. At least temporarily.

It was different the first three years, easier. He could hustle enough sales and rentals to pull it all together.

But the past year or so, with the oil crisis and other assorted disasters, tourism had fallen, the Yankee dollar was being hoarded back home. Uncle Sam was keeping a much more avid eye on dollar outflow. And Americans were scarcer.

Despite all these hazards, however, Nick knew he was working for the only boss he could get along with: himself. And working in the only place that made it possible: Monte Carlo.

He kept his vigil on Sheldon Bradley at the corner table. A man came to the bar and stood beside him. He ordered a "bourbon and ginger ale."

Nick recognized the familiar sounds, the music of Midwest America: out of habit (and hope) he quickly appraised his neighbor: the man's clothes suggested Mr. Straight. Still, one never knew. Nick played his customary opener: "You from the States?"

The man beamed as if Nick had divined a great mystery. "That's right. You too?"

A nod and into the next phase: Nick was a resident here and if there was anything he could do . . .

"Well, you wouldn't happen to know where I can pick up some films?"

"Films? No problem. Right across the park here— the Café de Paris."

"You really mean that?"

"Of course. They have everything. Black and white or—"

"Prefer color."

"They've got it all." Nick, the helpful fellow-American. "And they give you twenty-four hour developing service."

"No, no. That's not what I meant. I mean films. You know—ah—movies. Private movies, that is."

"Oh."

"Eight millimeter."

Nick had heard many requests in Monte Carlo but never for skinflicks or even porno postcards. He regarded the man quizzically. "I doubt if you can get them here. Have you tried Paris?"

"Maybe end of the month." A gulp of the bourbon and ginger ale. "Name is Babcock." Shaking hands. "Doctor Babcock." He was a dentist from Cincinnati. "Tell you," he was saying, "can't go home empty-handed. Promised the gang I'd bring back a few products made in France. For our Saturday bunch. We've got a grand group. Meet once a month, Saturday night, and run our films. Tell you—nothing like it to keep the old matrimonial wheels going and—"

"Excuse me—" A woman had appeared. "Harry, it's late if we're going to get in that trip to Nice—"

"Aw, come on, Janet—let's forget that. I thought I'd take us over to the Casino."

"Oh not again, Harry!" Mrs. Babcock was the kind of All-American female American men living abroad often hunger for.

The dentist introduced his wife, and Janet Babcock, upon learning that Nick lived in M.C., immediately declared: "Oh, aren't you lucky! I'd give anything to be able to live here—at least part of the year."

"Why don't you?" Nick felt it was only fair to inform the couple that he was in real estate.

"Oh, yes, why don't we indeed? . . . Just try to get my husband away. I worked on him for three years to get him on this trip."

"She's right," Harry Babcock admitted. "Well, nice to have met you, Mr. Nicholson. See you around."

"Goodbye. I certainly envy you," was Mrs. Babcock's farewell. But those nice, level midwest eyes conveyed to Nick that her farewell was a reluctant one.

"*Ciao,*" he said.

"What? Oh—yes. *Ciao.*" Janet Babcock repeated it, her smile was all there: no dentist could have had better advertising.

If he were left alone with her, Nick reflected, he

might well have convinced her to think of real estate. In fact if he were left alone with her the real estate might not even matter.

A fresh cigarette for luck. And then the encounter was forgotten. For now. Back to more vital concerns, back to the threesome at the corner table, Sheldon Bradley and the McFarlands. An odd combination: did fish of different fins swim together? There you had a socially impeccable cat like Sheldon Bradley mixing it up with John McFarland, one hell of a successful munitions manipulator, but a wildo:

But that was Monte Carlo—or rather the bar at the Hotel de Paris, which was in some ways probably not much different from the drugstore on Main Street, U.S.A. Everybody knew everybody and nobody could escape from anybody . . .

Ah, at last. The McFarlands were leaving, and as they passed, the lanky, restive, Irish-born weapons trader waved to Nick: "*Salem Maleikum.*"

"Hi, Johnny," Nick greeted him from the bar. "How's our friendly neighborhood merchant of death?"

"Surviving." McFarland chuckled.

Surviving. Some joke. A McFarland witticism: A few years back, Nick had learned, one of the fattest periods of McFarland's career was when he was the sweetheart of the CIA. It was McFarland who bought surplus arms from a Central American dictatorship and sold them to the rebel group. Point of story: originally the dictator got the arms free, courtesy of those mothers, the CIA; then sold them as surplus to McFarland, who, in turn, sold them to the rebel group of that same country.

In those days of secret operations McFarland didn't mind having his name linked with the CIA. It gave him a certain leverage and it definitely provided protection. But now that the agency had openly gone into the arms supply business, McFarland was on their shitlist.

Once when Nick had asked him how he felt about his trade in weapons, he'd replied: "The way I feel? What people do with the arms I sell them is not my business. Do you think car manufacturers feel responsible for traffic deaths? Something else, my friend—the amount I sell is small potatoes compared to the U.S.A. or France or Russia. Between them they've pumped trillions of dollars into the world arms market. They call it military aid. Jesus almighty, I'm only trying to make a living."

Nick went over to the corner table. "Hi, Sheldon," warmly to this man who was his only immediate prospect. "Mind if I join you until something tastier comes along?" He paid homage to Bradley the womanizer. Though obviously he didn't shine in this role as he had years ago—unless he was responding to the rejuvenating elixir of Simona's presence. Which he probably was. Just as Nick once had . . .

By any standard, given his generation, Sheldon Bradley was quite a dude. In his quiet, elegant way he exuded considerable machismo. If his nose was undistinguished or rather shapeless, he had a finely curved, bold mouth, gray eyes heavy-browed, and thick, longish hair, dark gray like pewter. He was constructed on narrow lines so that he appeared taller and thinner than his true dimensions.

He had to be ten or fifteen years older than he looked. He obviously took very good care of himself; that particular charm of his was more than cosmetic, it had to come from within. Sheldon Bradley was obviously a man for whom the finer things in life were imperative, and he knew how to use them. He probably was not, however, born with that proverbial silver spoon in his mouth, for he never spoke of his childhood or early years.

"Sit down, Nick." Sheldon Bradley readjusted the foulard ascot at the open collar of his pink, vintage Brooks shirt. On the table were his Cartier lighter and cigarette case, custom made (by Simona).

Sheldon Bradley was quality:

How many times, Nick recalled now, had he walked along Madison Avenue and passed that elegant five-story Georgian townhouse which bore the discreet signboard above the bow window: *Bradley & Mitchell, English and French Antiques.*

Five floors of the choicest. Plus warehouses. Plus cabinet and finishing shops in other parts of the city.

It was said that Bradley & Mitchell were to the world of fine furniture what Rolls-Royce was to the realm of motor cars. Bradley had assisted many millionaire connoisseurs in America as well as Europe in putting together their collections; he had acted as consultant to museums throughout the United States.

But currently Bradley was negotiating to sell out all his interests to his partner. Including that prime real estate, which Nick gathered must be worth an untidy sum of around five or six million quality dollars.

Five or six million added up to what? Went where?

To Geneva? To Monaco?

"You got yourself a faceful of sun today, Sheldon."

"Beach Club. Dozed off after two rubbers of bridge." Then: "I assume you have something by way of good news for me, Nick." The voice was cultivated. Eastern Establishment. With a foggy wisp of London SW1.

"Still not a thing available in that condo, Sheldon, but I've come across another building that—"

"Not interested, Nick."

"They've just begun this one, you can buy from plan in advance, write your own ticket. Thirty percent down and you own it while they're building. And if you should change your mind before completion, you can sell your interest and still come out ahead. And here prices go up by the hour."

"I can wait, Nick, I'm not in all that much of a hurry, you know."

You're not, baby, but I sure as hell am.

This year was certainly not the apogee of Nick's financial fortunes. Not only was real estate sluggish for someone like Nick who depended on the American dollar, but he was even in trouble on the most mundane levels, and since part of his popularity had always been due to his inflexible rule never to put the palm on rich friends (they were the most wary, the most paranoid), he was beginning to see his debt-list as in a bankruptcy petition:

1. He owed almost $100.00 to his friendly pharmacist;
2. He was behind at least $60.00 with his friendly laundry;
3. He owed $550.00 to his friendly dentist;
4. He owed three months' rental ($750.00) to his decidedly unfriendly landlord;
5. His $425.00 car insurance was due next month;
6. His Permit of Residence was up for renewal next September and he would have to provide the local authorities with a statement from his friendly banker guaranteeing that he was solvent and had enough funds to support himself.

"Sheldon—" from his shirt pocket Nick produced the

color brochure and passed it to Bradley. "This is the architect's sketch. There are several typical layouts. They promise key delivery September 1977."

Politely Sheldon perused the brochure, gave it back to Nick. "You know, it's curious. I can stroll down Fifth Avenue or Park today and have my pick of condominiums, and for half the price, I might add. Whereas here—I was just feeling out Johnny McFarland about his place, but alas—"

Goodchrist, into that same groove again: the Residence du Parc or nothing. Was there, Nick speculated, some psychological tic that made Bradley so obsessed with this one building? Was there something besides its sheer desirability—which was beyond debate? Or was it snobbism?

He was extremely fond of Sheldon Bradley. But sometimes he could be a pain in the ass when it came to his likes and dislikes. Nick recalled going to dinner with him a few times last summer, and Bradley always doing the same number: he got his blood pressure up if the table wasn't exactly where he ordered it, or if it was too close to another table or if the flowers were not fresh enough or carelessly arranged. "Tell me—what got you onto this *idée fixe*. Residence du Parc or nothing. Was it Simona?"

"No, no." But a casualness now, almost indifference. "It's simply—well, let's say—it's just my usual determination to get what I want. And once I settle here permanently it will have to be in that building."

Nick tried again. "If you want my advice, Sheldon,

forget the Residence du Parc. It's like the Académie Française—someone has to die before you can hope to get in."

"In that case, can't you arrange to have someone there killed off?" Bradley joked. "For example, someone who has an apartment on the thirtieth floor?"

"Look," Nick said, "don't think that's so funny. As a matter of fact, John McFarland's life insurance premium must come to a very ugly penny. Marie once told me there were at least eight gun runners murdered in Switzerland and Germany in the past few years. Did you know that?"

"Marie's mentioned it. But, as I told her, John is not in that same class, he's not some little gun smuggler taking stupid chances. John may have his devious way of operating but he's too smart to get himself into serious trouble."

"But he's not as kosher as someone like Sam Cummings, do you think?"

"Who is — as you put it — as 'kosher' as Cummings?"

Sheldon lit a cigarette. "You know, Nick, every time I see Cummings I feel he should have been a monsignor, or maybe a Jesuit priest, instead of president of Interarmco. After all, he's the biggest private arms trader around and he wouldn't give McFarland the time of day. Granted, John can be pretty rough and tough at times—though I can't help liking him. But never mind all that. Right now it's an apartment

I'm concerned with. I don't want a new building. I want an established one, and a person-to-person deal. There are also certain tax advantages—"

"Sheldon, if people like you keep trying to cut corners on your taxes how are we going to support the Pentagon and the CIA? You don't want to cramp our style in Washington, do you? They rely on guys like you to help them pay the rent." If Nick was teasing him now, instead of pushing business, it was because he was trying to change or alter Sheldon's rising impatience, a certain belligerence. Was it born out of his jealousy? Merely because Nick and Simona had been lovers back in the days of ancient history, Sheldon had these flare-ups of impatience, even a slight hostility: probably when or if he wasn't making it with Simona or if there'd been a battle. Nick felt one way to rid him of this was to get him laughing, ease him off, thaw the ice that still occasionally froze over their warm but tenuous friendship. And when you added business to friendship . . .

"The trouble with you, Sheldon, is you're a born winner."

"What are you, Nick—a born loser?"

"No, you've got it all wrong. I suppose what I am is a loser by choice, a pro. Listen, I'm not just your average flop, your average dilettante failure. Being a classy and contented loser is not easy, but I keep trying."

Bradley's smile was slow coming into play, the gray eyes showing the first glint of humor. Nick moved in at once. "Okay, don't worry. I'll get you the right condo."

"There's only one that's right, and you know what I mean."

"I have more than a vague idea, Sheldon, baby."

2

When Sheldon baby was a baby, his name was Samuel Bernstein. But, of course, that was long ago.

Yet now as he saw Nick peering at him there was that unwanted flash of memory and when it happened it could make him cringe with those black visions of the early days when he heard his German-born, greenhorn mother calling out to him affectionately in her Yiddish-Deutsch accent as he played in a neighborhood park with some of the kids: "Sam—Samela! Dinner—come *essen!*"

"SAMELA! SAMELA!" jeered one of the kids, each derisive syllable a whip of ridicule.

"Samela—" Another kid was at it, "don't forget to save me some of zat Cherman veener vurst!" Vicious, like those cartoons in the daily papers; for this was not long after World War I, and Detroit, like the rest of America back in those dark days, was still over-patriotic—anything German was smallpox. And as for anything Jewish, it was leprosy. (To Sam.)

Gangling Samela Bernstein was already outraged, mortified that he should be mocked for something in which he had no part, for which he had no mind, no heart— something for which he came to blame his mother. As for his father, he had died of pneumonia, complicated by diabetes. He did not remember him. Since his father was gone Sammy should have become the little man of the family, he should have been what all good Jewish boys were: the ideal son.

Sammy Bernstein's mother, Lily, had to work and she worked in Sheim's Department Store on Woodward Avenue; she was head saleswoman of the third floor, ladies' corsets.

Everyone at the store loved "Miss Lily."

And Sammy Bernstein hated everyone at the store.

"Sheldon—"

"Hmm?"

Sheldon Bradley leaped back to the present, the decidedly more agreeable present, from that pocked, red-brick housefront on Brush Street in Detroit to this brocade-paneled bastion, the cut-glass wall sconces in this most royal of all drinking parlors on the French Riviera.

"Be right back, Sheldon." Nick was on his feet.
"Let me catch Alma A—"

Sheldon saw her now. Alma Ainsworth had just
come in, tall and chesty and stately. Too stately, for
she was already half-stoned. She was accompanied
by Frederico Matossi, who had been a waiter in the
Rome Pavillon restaurant on East 53rd Street until he
was transported by the widow of a Detroit automobile executive to Monte Carlo. Since her demise
he had been freelancing and freeloading. Yet he had
a disarming honesty being the first to admit that men
were his sexual preference, though this did not seem
to inhibit his performance with women. For Alma,
whose husband shuttled on business between
Monaco and New York, he was an entertaining in-
terim companion . . .

Nick had returned, swift, lean and sandy-haired,
the dazzle of blue in his eyes dimmed: "No way,
Sheldon. Last time I saw Alma A she said she might
be moving back permanently to the States. Her
daughter was going to have a baby. First grandchild
and all that. But no way. Her daughter's had a mis-
carriage. So they're going to stay put in M.C." Nick
watched the woman as Frederico lit her cigarette. He
suggested a new possibility: Why shouldn't he discuss this matter with Frederico? In the first place
Frederico preferred life in New York. In the second
place Alma catered to him. And Nick recalled lover-
boy saying to him once: "Alma's got this gorgeous
townhouse on Sutton Place and she lets me use the

entire top floor. You know something, Nick — if it wasn't for Alma, I'd have to live on the West Side."

He asked Sheldon's opinion.

"From what I've observed," Sheldon answered, "when a woman falls in love with a piece of furniture or a painting, she can usually convince her husband to buy it for her."

Sheldon fingered his gold cigarette case. "What pleases me about the Residence du Parc is their high standard, not only the maintenance or upkeep, but the people who live there. First class."

"Would you say John McFarland is first class?"

"I meant in general. I don't imagine very many Jews live there." An uncalled for comment. But Sheldon had again yielded helplessly to those early memories of Detroit.

"Are you kidding, Sheldon? There's about as much anti-semitism in Monte Carlo as you'd find on the Grand Concourse in the Bronx."

What in God's name was the matter with him, at this late stage of the game. . . ?

He ordered a fresh round of drinks. The best was yet to come, wasn't it? In half an hour he would be driving up to Simona's in the hills.

Already he had banished his blackest thoughts, his absurd neurosis. Banishing what was disagreeable was the lucky syndrome Sheldon had been gifted with. Always had it, been forced to have it. He could be an indefatigable killer of time, a destroyer of the unbeautiful or the queasy, an executioner of all those figures of his boyhood:

As the nursery line had it, he would like to have said, if he could: I came, baby dear, out of the nowhere into the here.

3

Here and now the bronze beauty of the Residence du Parc rose thirty-five stories above the magnolia trees of the Casino park. On the corner terrace of the thirtieth floor there was a hiatus between phone calls —the telephone was John McFarland's lifeline.

"Tell me something, Marie—a while ago what was wrong with Sheldon, like he had a burr up his ass?" John McFarland asked his wife.

"Do you have to be vulgar? All the time?" She protested from the chaise longue. In irritation she brushed back a damp tendril of titian hair.

"If I'm vulgar you make it easy. And I thank you for it." McFarland gazed at her bikinied body, unmindful of the abrasiveness in her voice. He reached out to explore with his trigger-hard fingers the tenderness of Marie's thigh. "Care for a demonstration, flowerface?"

42

"Not now, please, John."

"Get to know me a little better, I'll let you call me Johnny." She was the only one who called him John. With everyone else it was always Johnny or Jack. Right. If he wasn't standing by for that call from Africa: That had gotten him hard as Marie, that call— one voice, the one he wanted to hear, had to hear.

Nevertheless he couldn't resist stirring, touching his wife with unabashed lechery:

Hand up between her legs. A hand on her (or a fist in anyone's face). Instinct, compulsion — that was Johnny. Not like his brother Clem, a Joycean scholar; not like his other brother Kevin, a film distributor in L.A. No, he had none of his mom in him (except her black eyes). He was all dad, who was a real stinger out of Ireland to New Jersey with zero in his pockets, and when he was laid to rest his estate was in the big numbers.

Until the tax bite came.

Same way now with Johnny. The case pending with the IRS. They wanted him to liquidate his Canadian company: if he lost the right it would cost him about one-million-six, plus fines, for undeclared income. Plus legal fees.

A crying shame. For the way his circuit went it was ideal. Let's say—as he oversimplified it for Marie— he bought weapons from England he would im- mediately sell them (on paper) for a small profit to his Canadian company (and pay taxes on that small profit to England and Uncle Sam) who would then (again on paper) sell them for another marginal profit to his Monaco company (paying taxes on that marginal profit to Canada and Uncle Sam). And his Monaco company would sell and bill these weapons at a 100-500 percent profit to the originally committed buyer (now, however, no taxes to Monaco, no taxes to Uncle Sam).

This circuit would close off if he lost the case and had to shell out to the IRS. Johnny got hot flushes and scratchy palms at the mere thought of what this could mean. It would also put him in a cash bind; and in this business it was the man who could pay spot cash who got the hottest weapons deals. Say one of your agents cued you into a bid for old or surplus weapons in Spain — a deal John had once put through, acquiring 100,000 pieces, including German Mausers, Italian VV70 sniper rifles and Remington rolling blocks, along with thousands of pistols. Had he not had cash in hand, that transaction would have exploded in his cherry-red Irish face. . . .

Even so, it was still more than just buying and selling. It was something else John had, always had had: a true love.

Johnny, age ten, found it one summer afternoon, this gem, this true love: a Whitworth Express rifle, African series, with that stock of dense-grained English walnut, solid steel recoil bearing cross bolt, in the attic of his dad's house. And the love affair began that day. Soon he was ecstatically dismantling the gun and reassembling it. His passion proliferated, churned through his blood.

For the Korean War he was drafted but never had to get into combat, though he wanted to. Since he had come to know more about the world's arms than anyone in his army group he was made a gun instructor. And afterward he was hired by the CIA, identifying classified foreign weapons.

Witnessing the way arms were acquired, discarded, sold or left to rust away, he borrowed capital from his dad and before he was twenty-three was doing a land-office business in small arms, rifles, grenades, uniforms, a mail order business which expanded its volume until 1968 (when it looked as if that Gun Control Act, banning importation of military arms, would be passed) and he sold out and paid a money-dealer five percent to get the loot out of the States and over to Switzerland.

So it began.

Today it was different. The operation now was big, like his payroll, and big like the kind of payoffs he had to give generals or defense ministers in virtually every country on the African continent: like the one due next week, his biggest deal, the daddy of them all.

And something else. He had to travel. Far and wide.

And he had to do it alone.

Not with a woman. Not with Marie.

Not that he was losing any sleep. For he had the gold sweat of his love's labor boxed up right here in M.C. and in Geneva.

Also he'd put a chunk into this condominium: and there were worse places he could have put a quarter of a million dollars into than the Residence du Parc. Worth double that sum today. The co-owners were all smartass elegant. But he only fell into it because Marie was a Monégasque and the builder knew her family. Right?

Right.

Ahh, tighter up between her legs now.

Umm. She no like? Okay. "Your trouble is you've been getting too much. I've spoiled you."

She stirred again. "There was nothing wrong with Sheldon except that I think he thinks you are too vulgar."

McFarland picked up the magazine on his lap, *World Weapons,* dropped it to the marble floor, thus exposing the open fly of his plaid shorts, private parts visible to the summer sky: the bulge of the cartridge chamber with the barrel aiming upward. "What's this vulgar kick lately? I notice when Nick is vulgar, that's okay."

"Nick is amusing. You are just vulgar vulgar. And Sheldon Bradley gets almost fidgety when you're around. It would not do you any harm to watch him. Wouldn't do you any harm at all, John."

"The way I am, you love me for it. Come on, Marie, come on, lovie." At first when he'd met her she'd seen him for what he was, a real live natural man, a ballsy guy who was always himself, right? She truly admired him. But lately she seemed to be put off by the very qualities she had married him for.

"All right. Sheldon Bradley is a gentleman. Fine. But do we have to make a national issue of it?" Jesus almighty, she could sound off like bad news sometimes, bad as the U.S. Congress finally passing that Gun Control Act back in 1968, about as welcome as that.

"John, you're the one who is always asking Sheldon for drinks, not me."

"I like to keep a connection like him hot. He's got plenty stashed around here, or at least he's going to have after he quits the States. When he's here permanently I want him to know he's got a friend in John McFarland. And vice versa. Never know. Even dumb squirrels stash chow away for a winter's meal, right?"

Marie broke the freeze, smiled at him — that green-eyed smile, and that fine hair!

The telephone.

"Your call, John."

He was up and striding around the corner of the terrace to the east end: the office section was separate from the rest of the apartment, separate halls, doors, phones. And no one but himself ever used those office phones, or answered them. Separate safes. And no one but he knew the combinations. No employees here, no assistants. Here it was all McFarland.

"Yes?"

"Mr. McFarland, telex for you."

It was Helene's voice from M.C. Business Services. But this was not what he'd been waiting for. "Okay. Shoot, Helene."

Six years ago, the voice had been Marie's. She too had worked for Monte Carlo Business Services (secretaries, translators, computers, teletype, telex, mimeographing). That's how it had happened. Telex for you Mr. McFarland, and after Marie had read it to him he'd asked that it be sent right over. But no messenger at hand, and so Marie had delivered it herself, and next morning at 8:30 who called M.C. Business Services, no one but your "friendly merchant of death," John McFarland, asking for Marie, asking her for lunch.

No deal.

Dinner?

Deal.

After that evening, with local girl making out in the Grill atop the Hotel de Paris (some men of her Monégasque family had been working for the hotel or the Casino for a hundred years; her uncle was a croupier, and she had a brother who was in the police, the business-suit secret police). It took John thirty days to complete the deal: marry her.

Helene started reading the telex to him now. In English. From Barcelona. John kept his lighter hanging from a leather thong around his neck. Always handy. He lit a cigarette, listened. It was not the message he'd been waiting for, not from Africa. "Okay, Helene, thanks. Send it over."

The phone rang again. Now. This was it. "Yes? Willy?" He reached down, pressed the lever that turned on the scrambler. Unnecessary most times, but why take chances. If a tap was on him, they'd have to sweat to unscramble the conversation. "Okay, Willy. Go ahead with it as planned." Then: "How's that Gulf shipment of Stens? Okay, you meet with those Ubangis? And? Okay. Yes, you meet me at the airport. Okay?" He listened intensely, lit another cigarette. Then: "But what about the initial order — the 80mm mortar ammo? Certainly we can deliver. Make it a package, and make it fast. Get the top price without losing the deal. Okay. No, I'll send him a postcard. Thanks, Willy. *Salem Maleikum.*" He rang off with the familiar Moslem farewell or greeting: *Peace be with you.*

He turned to his Olivetti electric and picked a post-card from the pile, color shot of the Monte Carlo Casino and the park grounds, inserted it into the machine and typed up, in his cryptic brief style, the confidential information.

Only five of his key agents around the globe knew how to read these messages. McFarland knew that postcards got through when regular mail didn't. In some countries authorities checked foreign envelopes but cards were never bothered with. Even in the case of mail embargo or a bomb scare: postcards got delivered.

John picked up cards in airports all around the world. He loved gaudy and bawdy postcards. One day last week he was out taking a walk, dropping a batch of cards into the mailbox on the Boulevard des Moulins and had run into Sheldon Bradley, and Bradley needling him gently: "Why do postcards always have to be so tacky, John? How can you use them? But you can't go by me. I wouldn't waste postage on them."

John could understand Sheldon's attitude. No feelings hurt. He can laugh.

John liked to laugh and he liked to send his gay and gaudy postcards with their heavy fire-powered messages.

Back to Marie: She was reading a book, she had become one hell of a reader since all his traveling. That's the way to keep 'em. Pregnant or reading.

If he'd made a mistake with Marie it was marrying her. She was not easy to leave. He should have married someone who didn't matter, leave her when he had to and forget about it.

Not with Marie.

Jesus almighty, he could be cool and controlled when he did business. But sometimes at night in those air-conditioned hotel rooms in Africa he would break out in the hots thinking about Marie, worrying, crazy with worry and with want and love and wanting her. . . .

His mistake was in choosing too well.

He leaned over her now and his tongue touched the hollow just under her ear, she liked that. Or she used to. He came around and edged himself down on the chaise and kissed her and his hand was again cupping the insides of her thigh:

So right, and he always knew when anything felt right. Like the heft of a pistol, say a Mauser Parabellum, with that pressed walnut grip against the palm. (See your M & M Sporting Man's Catalogue: order it now, Model P-08, basic design of Georg Luger, all parts forged and precision machined. First production of Parabellum since World War II, re-established by the great Mauser-Werke facilities in Oberdorf, West Germany. Also available complete line of Nazi decorations, medals, ribbons. . . .)

He stretched out beside Marie and murmured as of yore: "'tis McFarland's night, sweet and right, 'tis McFarland's night."

4

It was a Sunday in late June; and like most summer Sundays, Nick left his apartment mid-morning and drove to the beach to see what fish might be had for frying.

And, as always, he drove via the harbor area to check out which of the off-shore tax-dodging sailors were in town for a bit of landlubbing. Today that white Moby Dick of naval architecture, Niarchos's newest Greek toy, the world's greatest private yacht, the *Atlantis*, was there. (Can you imagine, folks, how poor Ari and Jackie must have felt when they first saw it? Made the *Christina* look like a Chris-Craft, no?)

But oh for that freewheeling international independence; just a little bit of all that gold for Nick and he could realize that undreamlike dream: when, with a little help of a few friends, he'd be able to take that U.S. passport of his and throw it right back at those wonderful folks who gave you the murders of the brothers John and Robert, and Martin Luther, and who killed my wife and child. Yes, the same people who gave you Vietnam, Santo Domingo, Chile, and that super box-office entertainment, Watergate. And those living dolls at the CIA who give you all that free service—open your mail, tap your phone, check out your garbage, analyze your urine . . .

He turned into the lower road, the Avenue du President Kennedy which led to the section running beneath the Hotel de Paris, the Casino, the towering Residence du Parc—no, Sheldon, I haven't forgotten you, Baby. Eastward on the Avenue Princess Grace he sped in his old TR 3, top down, his fair hair roughed by the current of sea air. Onward and eastward, passing the extension of reclaimed land on which sat Nirvana for Swingers, the circular Summer Sporting Club, and on beyond to the grounds of the Monte Carlo Bath and Beach Club:

"The Monte Carlo Bath and Beach Club, folks," Nick might have said on his tour-bus spiel, "is indeed something else. Bailey's Beach in Newport it is not. Nor is it the Meadowbrook in Southampton. Being exclusive is a luxury better suited to a great democracy like America. Here in the Old World, folks, even in a princely sovereignty like Monaco, the beach club is simultaneously chic and ordinary: for one and all. All you have to do is pay. Rent a tent by the month. If you can afford the tab. But even without a tent, without a nickel, you can sit on the beach or water's edge, you can swim. The law here has it that the shoreline belongs to the people. . . .

"What we have here at this club, folks, is a community of smart charcoal-and-white striped tents set in a row, each tent commodious enough to contain a family: hubby, wifey and kiddies, and maybe a sheik or two.

"What we have here, folks, is service: from ice-cream cones to champagne lunches. To paraphrase the old Basin Street Blues, it's here at this club where de plain and de fancy folks meet."

Nick did not rent a tent here — after all he was neither insane enough nor solvent enough—he only dropped in to rap with friends, to check on new arrivals and, hopefully, come across a lead for a possible realty transaction. . . .

As he passed through the entry, the club's director greeted him with the kind of cordiality reserved for the paying gentry. In his long-practiced English he told him that a man had come by looking for him.

Who?

A Mr. Grant.

Grant? The only Grant Nick knew of was Ulysses S. Did he say what he wanted?

No. Just that he was from the United States Consulate in Nice.

And Nick now recalled that twice this past week he had noticed the same figure in the same car, a bald man at the wheel. It was completely crazy to think anyone would be following him. Yet he'd had this gut feeling.

But who the hell would want to tail him?

What, he asked the director, did this cat look like?

Very American. Beige. Drip-dry. Bald. At the bar.

Nervously, Nick decided to make a pass at the bar, a recessed area behind the last row of tents. But he was just a fraction too nervous. He walked around the beach for a while, waving salutations as he passed the various tents:

Tent 88: Mr. and Mrs. John McFarland.

Tent 82: Mr. Sheldon Bradley (Simona with him today).

Tent 61: Mr. and Mrs. Herbert Ainsworth (no Herbert today, only Alma A and Gorgeous Frederico).

He turned back and made his second pass at the bar: yes, he singled him out at the far end, a man in tan pants and tan shirt, thin, Baldy himself, drinking a daring Schweppes tonic.

"I understand" — Nick settled himself on the adjoining stool—"you were looking for me."

"Yes. Sorry to trouble you on a Sunday. But I have to leave tomorrow and, well, that's unimportant."

From his wallet he withdrew a small card and handed it to Nick:

HAROLD GRANT

Internal Revenue Service

Division of European Operations

No address, no telephone.

"I understand you're from the U.S. Consulate in Nice."

"No—just use it as a base when I'm in the area. As I was saying, Mr. Nicholson—please let me apologize. What'll you have to drink?"

"Nothing, thanks." Acid was already forming in his insides. "Mind if I ask you what you—"

"I'm sure, Mr. Nicholson, you might be able to guess." Grant spoke quietly, with patience and courtesy. "Among other matters, we want to discuss 1967."

Had to come sooner or later. But why couldn't it have come later?

"Our records show that you chose not to pay twenty percent of your taxes that year because you claimed it went into the Vietnam war. That deduction was arbitrary on your part and of course illegal. And our records also show that since that year you have not filed at all."

"1967 was my only big income year." Nick heard himself indulging in the rueful non sequitur.

"Tell me something— " Grant with his clean-cut

Nordic features resembled a hairless President Gerald Ford "—tell me something. Were you serious about that? Did you really believe you and all the others could hinder the war effort by withholding your taxes?"

"Let's just say that for me it was an irresponsible phase of youth, Mr. Grant, purely an impish impulse, irresponsible, and un-American. Is that why you're here to see me?"

"Indirectly, yes."

"Well, good. It's a relief to know you people are sparing no efforts, coming all the way to Monte Carlo to track down major crooks like me."

"You've got a nice sense of humor, Mr. Nicholson. It's one of the qualities that I understand people in Monaco admire you for. And it's a real plus as far as Washington is concerned."

"How much is it I owe? Some astronomical figure like three thousand bucks?"

"Three thousand eight hundred and fifty-nine dollars and sixteen cents, to be precise, Mr. Nicholson."

Grant started revolving his glass of tonic on the bar's surface. "What we wanted to discuss with you is this: We're interested in a profile study of the American community here."

"Meaning what?"

"Simply profiles: life style, habits, associations, where they go when they leave Monaco. Simple, general information, that's all." A friendly smile.

"Oh, sh—shucks, I was hoping you were about to

make me an honorable, derring-do double agent, something I've always wanted to be."

Grant smiled. "There are some Americans here who seem to have no visible means of support, if you follow me. And Washington expects citizens to pay their dues. Too many of them like to use the club but they don't like to pay their dues. They like to wave that passport but not salute the flag. If you can give us some leads, leads that we're looking for, our department is prepared to forget your Vietnam — your 'youthful phase', and in addition you can count on five hundred dollars a month deposited in your bank account."

Nick was not ready for this. It had to be some kind of joke, some kind of put-on. It was so nutty and incredible that Nick had to challenge him: "Could you make it more like a thousand?"

"Perhaps."

"Tax free?" Nick still couldn't believe it. This couldn't be happening to him. Not to Harper Nicholson.

But why not? It came to him immediately now — that newspaper piece from the New York *Times* reported in the *Herald Trib* over here. He'd read it aloud to John McFarland and they had both laughed and later he had clipped it out and slipped it between the pages of his passport. Parts of it he could quote virtually verbatim:

Miami, March 16 (NYT) A Miami woman has said that she was recruited by the Internal Revenue Service in

1972 to take part in a widespread operation to gather information on the sex life and drinking habits of thirty prominent south Floridians. . . .

She said that the overall goal of the operation had never been made very clear to her but that she had been promised a lifelong pension of $20,000 a year and a home abroad if she could come up with information that would "get" them . . .

It was like a small CIA operation, she asserted. "I was supposed to mingle in local exclusive clubs and bars . . . pick up all the dirt I could . . . maybe even to go to bed with them . . . ."

The Internal Revenue Service normally gathers intelligence only on tax violations. In Washington . . .

"Mr. Grant, are you sure you are talking to the right guy? Unsavory business like this?"

"It is not at all unsavory," the man answered at once, and with righteous indignation. "We think of it as a service to your country. I know you might laugh at that. But I can assure you there are many respectable, decent Americans who help the department with its profiles."

"So you're convinced I'm your man? Well, let me tell you — right here and now, sir" — Nick turned to the bartender and ordered a double Scotch on the rocks. He lit a cigarette, inhaled too deeply and coughed — "Okay, Mr. Grant, if that's what you think, let's get this straight. If you think I'm the kind of person who'd stoop to something like this, then let me tell you right here and now: I am."

Mr. Grant smiled, tipped his head sidewise, his naked pate ashine with goodwill. "I appreciate your way of putting things, Mr. Nicholson."

As if obliged to answer himself, Nick said: "Unfortunately timing is in your favor, Mr. Grant. I'm presently in a tight corner."

"Yes, we know."

Yes, we have done our homework, haven't we?

"At any rate, Mr. Nicholson, if you'd like to think about it, if you'd like more time, that's agreeable with us. I'll call you at your apartment a week from tomorrow. Say, at nine. Is that okay with you?"

It was too easy. Too tricky. "What do I do — just check out all the boys on your shitlist?"

"No, we know about the obvious ones. It's the others we're interested in. And that we will leave up to you. You're acquainted with all the Americans living here, or most of them. We'll trust you to put us on the right tracks."

"I happen to have a few very good friends here."

"We aren't insisting that you compromise personal friends, Mr. Nicholson. We try to be understanding."

The sonofabitch, Nick raged, was making it near impossible for him to turn down this thoroughly immoral proposition! The bastard was giving him all that leeway, and all that money! . . .

A week from tomorrow Grant would call and ask for Nick's decision: would it be a noble NO? Maybe he'd better let the slot machines decide this one: if he pulled a mixed zero, it would be No; if he yanked down a handful or a jackpot, it would be Yes. In that way the decision would be off his back and spare him sleepless nights.

Nick started back to tentville. He turned into the second row. He saw, strutting seaward from tent 61, Alma A's golden Frederico, leaping into the water, great arms and shoulders a challenge to the forces of nature.

A good time to move in on him. Nick swam out after the sexual acrobat. (Frederico told the story on himself: when he was born, when his father first beheld his babyhood pecker, he had exclaimed, "This boy is never going to have to work a day in his life!")

Breathless, Nick came abreast of him. "Listen, Frederico, want to talk to you. Important. Private."

"Sure, Nick." They trod water for a while and then slowly headed back to shore, where they stood on fine soft sand that not God but the trucks of Prince Rainier had wrought.

"You say it's private?" Frederico brought those dark boyish eyes to bear on tent 61.

"What I want to discuss with you—" Nick decided to be swift, direct and unsubtle. "Would you be interested in picking up an easy five thousand bucks?"

"Sure. What's the hitch?" Frederico tugged at his trunks which of course fit snug as a jock strap.

"No hitch. I have a client who's hung up on the Residence du Parc and I want to sell him Alma's apartment."

"She isn't selling."

"But if you could convince her to change her mind I could make my deal and you'd get yourself five thou for your good work."

Frederico frowned. "I don't know, Nick."

"Well, I had this idea that you've got a lot of clout when it comes to Alma A. Maybe I'm wrong."

"Why would she suddenly sell? Her daughter lost that baby—Alma's put a fortune into that apartment, decorators, architects, the works. It's gorgeous, that place."

"She'd sell for one reason, Frederico."

"What's that?"

"Well, for five thousand dollars can't you come up with one good reason?"

The dark eyes were abruptly afire with greed, also with puzzlement. "What the hell do I say to her? 'Hey, Alma, why don't you sell this crummy joint and'—and what?"

"Maybe," Nick improvised, "you are suddenly unhappy living right here in the center of M.C., all that traffic and all those tourists. Maybe you long for the simple life—"

"I hate the simple life."

"Look, Frederico, if you convince Alma to unload the apartment and to buy a villa in the hills—that could mean an *additional* five thousand for you."

"She's too smart."

"I happen to know of one villa that would be hard to resist. Very modern, contemporary. Chic. And it cantilevers straight out from the cliff."

"Can't what?"

"It cantilevers—juts out, supported by concrete. A show place."

"Okay, Nick. I'll feel her out."

"Feel her up."

"Nothing like that, Nick. We have a play — you know, a play-tonic relationship." Frederico gave him a friendly thump on the chest and turned, ran, and dove back into the water, providing a spectacular performance, superstud at sea.

On to tent 82, Simona and Sheldon; they were facing each other across a backgammon board. Bad timing. He'd take off and drop in on the McFarlands a few tents beyond.

"Nick, don't rush off. Come sit down, we just finished a beautiful game," Sheldon said.

"Meaning he won," added Simona.

Nick stood by the table. "I wanted to tell you, Sheldon, I just had a talk with Frederico, baby."

Sheldon, basking in the sun of Simona's presence, was a different man and he could be, in his muted way, an amusing one. "I trust—and the pun is intended—that your talk was fruitful."

Simona tilted back in her chair and smiled.

"Maybe," Nick said.

"What are you up to now, Nicky — sounds like pimping," Simona observed cheerfully. Even now, thirty-four years after she had been born, the faint echo of Dallas, Texas, persisted. When he had first met her in New York that accent was definable, though she made a vain if conscientious effort to kill it. He was sitting beside her in the reception room of the Ford model agency and he'd said: "Texas. Very deep in the heart of. Correct?"

"Ah was hopin you wouldn't say it. Ah was tellin mahself, ah sure hope this man doesn't make a horse's ass of himself, and now you've gone and done just that."

Less than a month later they were living together, traveling together, working together, selling their brand-name employers' jewels and clothes right off their backs and fingers. It was easy going at first; he and Simona always had an easy relationship, the vibrations were good, no possessiveness, no excess of sentimentalities; they were good dinner partners and better bed partners. . . .

Yet they seemed to be going nowhere. Nick knew it. Simona knew it. One day at The Breakers in Palm Beach they were lying by the pool baking out a hangover from a party the night before (commissions on their sales were over thirteen hundred dollars by the time they'd put down the last brandies) and Simona had abruptly said: "I can't stand much more of this, Nicky. It's fine, it's fun. But it's shit."

He'd agreed. Where could they go from here? He had no idea. He couldn't find a niche for himself. But he perceived Simona's potential: why couldn't she get into something like jewelry? She was good with her hands and had built-in good taste. They discussed it. And as soon as they returned to New York she enrolled in a goldsmithing class. She had found her true métier. "It took you, Nicky, as always, to push me in the right direction. You're the only guy who knows what I'm like, and you're the only guy I could ever really talk to. Including my father . . .

Looking at her now, he thought once again that the years had been better to her than to any woman he'd known. To begin with, Simona had that resilient Texas frame, that beef-fed health, to which you add yoga, organic foods and a discipline never to help yourself to a second helping, and you had one considerable broad.

And that pale gold hair that she wore in a bold chignon gave her a particular distinction. It was no puzzle what turned Sheldon Bradley on. . . .

Nick had been present on the occasion when Sheldon first met Simona in New York, the infamous day in 1970 when Nixon ordered the United States forces into Cambodia.

A dinner party, and Sheldon in black tie was sitting

next to a white-clad Simona, who was still sporting the clothes and jewels of her employers. Sheldon was admiring one of her gold rings, and Simona with champagne tongue said she could make one as good if not better:

Would she make one for Sheldon? He wanted to give a special Christmas present to his partner's wife.

Simona had looked at Sheldon Bradley and broken out in that throaty, Rabelaisian laugh: "*Partner's* wife. I've heard men saying they want to buy a gift for a 'young niece' or a 'secretary' or a 'daughter' — but a 'partner's wife'? Mr. Bradley, you've just got to be a comedian!"

Sheldon Bradley never bought the ring for Grace Mitchell. And he never managed to see Simona. He called her several times, but it was a period in her life when she was so caught up in the New York social current she was never free when he was.

Of course in those days she only *talked* about being a goldsmith. It wasn't until Simona quit her jobs and after she and Nick broke up and she went to Monaco and bought that cottage in the hills that she perfected her craft as a goldsmith. Now she was producing her original designs for which she had acquired a number of private and commercial buyers. (Nick from time to time would turn up with some prospective customer and even accept a commission if Simona made a sale or received an order.)

As for the *haute couture* clothes that Sheldon, like most everyone else, admired, she had given them all the toss — nowadays she seldom wore anything except bleached-out jeans and T-shirts. People, however, still took a long look when she passed. . . .

How come, Nick asked himself, as he viewed her in the tent now, how come he had never married her? The answer, if there was one, was that they probably had lived too much too quickly.

No. The answer was that he'd met Jane.

Jane. She was exactly what he wasn't looking for: someone without whom he couldn't possibly live, breathe, exist:

But there she'd been in that afternoon drizzle standing right in front of him during that rally protesting the invasion of Cambodia. . . .

Jane in that shiny, floppy black rain hat and that shiny black slicker, her sunny hair damp and straight and long, her big eyes ablaze with fury as the cop pushed her back behind the barrier at the curb, and the way she refused to be manhandled, and jutting her middle finger upward in the familiar gesture of defiance.

He'd walked her to the brownstone where she lived. But suddenly she ran ahead, up the stairs of the stoop, her face ashen, contorted. "Excuse me — sick—hot dog—got the trots—sorry—"

After this romantic encounter he returned the next evening and spent a long while talking or trying to talk with her, for part of the time she was in the bathroom, her diarrhea persisting. Between these junkets to the john she told him she hadn't gone to work that day. She worked in a travel agency, she did the manager's job and received a secretary's salary. Her boss was on the comp list for all those cruises and package tours, but she never got beyond the office.

Where would she have liked to go?

Europe. Italy. France. England. Greece. Germany.

He wasn't going to tell her he'd covered most of that ground. On her walls were all those travel posters, including one of Monte Carlo, and he didn't have the heart to tell her he'd also been there and how pissed off he was. You couldn't do that to Jane.

Jane Buchanan had been twenty-two years old when he met her, and twenty-two-years-and-two-months when they got married. He moved into her small brownstone walk-up and while she worked he looked for a job. At five-thirty each evening he would call for her at the travel agency:

And often by six-thirty they'd tumbled into bed, and for Nick it was as if he had never known another woman or maybe it was as if he had known too many or maybe it was a whole new kind of chemistry. Unlike the earthy Simona, Jane seemed to exist in a gossamer world:

Her body was slim, her sexual appetite wasn't. In sentimental moments he tended to regard her as a kind of mischievous angel. Their bed life certainly was marked by spontaneity. There were evenings of acrobatics. He would lift her lithe body onto him and holding her thus get off the bed and move with her around the bedroom, or he would carry her into the living room, her thighs clamped tight around him, his grip cocksure, and she would sound off with delight as he hoisted her up onto the top of the upholstered armchair and bracing himself, still inside her, he would stand against her, her breasts touching his chest, and he would make wondrous love to her. . . .

"That's the way they do it in Istanbul," Jane once said.

"How do you know?"

"I don't, Nick. But that's how I just thought of it."

Nick found himself sharing her pleasure in all the travel posters on her walls as well as the collection of books and travel guides from early Baedeker to modern Michelin, and the scrapbook of postcards from Europe sent to her by friends or classmates from Hunter College. . . .

For someone who had never gone further than Grand Canyon, she must have been the original travel freak. And her pregnancy in no way inhibited her. If they could only get out of the States and live somewhere in Europe, raise the baby in a kind of international style. "It ought to be bi- or tri-lingual. I'm taking French at Berlitz and after that I'm going into Italian and Spanish." She would sit in a lotus position in jeans and an old shirt of his, and she would talk for hours: she was as dead earnest about these fantasies of hers as she was about Washington politics:

What a creature was Jane, what a criminal injustice

that she never lived even long enough to apply for a passport. . . .

What a creature was she, and how protective, right out of a comic strip, Nick had been when her belly began to show that the baby was real, really real, inside her. And Nick's life took on a whole new dimension, it was all totally new and original, it had never happened to any living man before, loving someone like this and knowing you were going to be a father and that this earnest winsome girl was actually going to produce a child. His child. "It's absolutely underwhelming," he used to shout out after the second or third drink.

He had followed the obstetrician's advice: every night before they went to sleep he would sit on the bed beside her, lift her nightgown and rub her distended stomach with cocoa butter. "It'll help prevent postnatal scars," the doctor had counseled.

"Do you know, Nick"—she would say as he gently rubbed in the cocoa butter—"that you can take a boat trip down the Rhine and within only a few hours you can pass the castle of—"

No matter if it was the Rhine or a French canal or a palazzo in Venice, she could exuberantly bring to it all the knowledge and ambience of one who'd been there for many years, and she made you hate yourself for not having gone to these places or not having properly appreciated them if you'd already been there. . . .

And the night of her murder he'd found her body

lying amid all those travel brochures scattered, some
bloody, on the floor . . . .

"You were saying, apropos Frederico—?" Sheldon
inquired, and reached over to light Simona's
cigarette.

"I took your suggestion, Sheldon," Nick answered,
"but I still wonder just how much influence this
schmuck really has on old Alma A—"

Sheldon's attention had drifted back to the backgammon board. "What can I give you by the way of a
drink, Nick?"

Nick declined. He had to be going.

Sheldon was always gracious and though he went
out of his way now to be a host, Nick knew that
something seemed to happen to him whenever he
saw Nick and Simona together. It was best to be with
Sheldon alone.

"*Ciao.*" He started out of the tent.

Simona blew him a kiss. "So long, you adorable
shit."

5

"You know" — Sheldon started setting up the back-gammon board—"you have a way of saying anything and making it sound—to use an antiquated word—ladylike."

Her gaze was loving. "That's my problem, Sheldon. Underneath it all I'm just a fucking lady. As Nick used to say."

"Very funny."

"Sorry. I meant it to be that, nothing more."

"Yes." But Sheldon could never quite bring himself to dwell on Simona and Nick, not in any explicit way. Each reminiscence about their past life nipped him, a bee sting on his psyche.

Yet his feelings, his acceptance of Simona's decidedly earthy personality—this represented a definite step forward for him.

Though he still was made uncomfortable by those Yiddish expressions Nick was so fond of using, those phrases he'd picked up from that friend of his, Hy Greenspan.

"You want to make love, that's your trouble, darling." In the tent Simona suddenly paused mid-game. "I can tell. You're not concentrating."

He glanced at the backgammon board. "You've got a dirty mind and you're clairvoyant." He rose and went around and kissed her.

"You've got an absolutely delicious erection, Sheldon."

"If I hadn't already ordered lunch—"

"Why don't we cancel it?"

"Yes—the only thing—I really don't approve of that. I made quite a fuss in there before and I'm sure they're going to special trouble—"

"To hell with it. You always make quite a fuss. Stop being so damn proper. We're going back to the house." Simona was on her feet and swiftly into her old frayed jeans and T-shirt.

By the time Sheldon drove her up into the hills above Monte Carlo close to the eastern border of France, the sky had taken on a brooding cast. "Looks definitely like rain," he said as they went into her Mediterranean cottage. "I feel better now about canceling that lunch."

The rain turned out to be more than a Riviera

shower. The black clouds above the ridges of Mount Agel erupted and a strong wind developed, sweeping in a sibilant rush across the stands of pines.

Simona's house was low and its tile roof sloped against the hillside; the house was protectively flanked by two ancient and fragrant eucalyptus trees.

As they went inside Sheldon was reminded of the first summer he had come to Monte Carlo and had tracked her down here.

She'd appeared at her door wearing old jeans and a denim apron and her gloved hands were holding a gold bracelet she was in the midst of polishing. There was a black smudge on her cheek. She recognized him immediately: "If you're still looking for a ring for your partner's wife, I'll be pleased to make one for you."

In a single instant she had evoked a night long past: he had been struck that first time he'd met her at that New York dinner party, not only by her elegance but by the extent of traveling she'd done for someone her age, the places she and Nick had been in the course of their young and peripatetic lives. Simona's close presence on that evening had been hard for him to cope with, Simona in that severe white gown and the mass of fair hair. . . .

He recalled now how absurdly critical he'd once been of this house, though since then he'd come to hold an affection for it. Simona had bought it at a fair price that included most of the furniture, good, simple French provincial pieces, and she'd added two Eames chairs and a glass/chrome coffee table; the whiteness of the rough-textured walls was relieved by the contemporary lithographs she'd acquired over the years, having known or met most of the artists. The old dining room, which faced the garden, was now her workshop: the heart of the house.

On that first visit he'd realized he was looking at a distinctly different Simona than the one who had originally inspired his infatuation. . . . She had become a down-to-earth, barefooted boss of her own cottage industry. She was now bored by the entire syndrome of her past life, the people or the fashions that were "in" or "out." "I just can't work myself up about all that shit any more," she announced to him with that ladylike smile.

The first summer he took her out at least once a week. He was understanding when she'd told him she had had an affair that was a disaster, an affair with a local doctor who commuted daily to his wife in Antibes. "He was six-feet-six and bad news right down to his toes."

The evening before he was to fly back to New York Sheldon had decided it was finally the propitious moment to tell her everything he'd been thinking, and that he was going insane with love for her. . . .

"Why did you wait until now to tell me all this?" Simona had demanded with an almost fierce indignation.

Because he wasn't sure how she would take it and also she was, after all, quite a bit younger than he was.

"Yes, I know—" she'd said, "I'm young enough to be your partner's wife." Then: "Do you think, after all the idiots, all the fucked-up, immature married men I've had to get involved with or escape from . . . if you think I'm letting you get on that plane tomorrow, you're just out of your antique-picking mind. You're not even going to get out of this house."

He got out of the house a few times, of course. But for most of the two weeks he'd stayed there he scarcely left her bed.

"Tell me the truth, Simona," he'd teased her a year later. "What is it about me that you find so 'irresistible'?"

"You really want to know? No matter what I say?"

"I won't hold it against you."

"I wish you would," came her cheerful reply, and she'd kissed him. "Well, all right. Here goes. You made it with me right away because you didn't try to make it with me right away. You never gave me that quick heavy pitch the first time we met or when you knocked on my door that first summer you came here. I mean, all my life I've turned off the minute a guy gave me that immediate invitation to the sexual waltz. And something else. This is terribly elegant: I happen to hate it when a man leaves the toilet seat up after he pees; it's a funny feeling suddenly sitting on that cold porcelain. But you always put the seat back down when you're through and that, lover, is what I call consideration."

She'd said, oh yes, there were other things about him: like the way he would bring her a single perfect rose instead of a great clump. Or the way he would arrive at the house sometimes and stand at the door and quietly say, "I have a little love for you."

"You know something else, Sheldon? Whenever I wake up in the middle of the night or early morning and just slightly touch you, you always respond to me. No matter how tired or groggy you may be. You're always ready to listen or talk about whatever I'm stewing or dreaming about, and you always put your arms around me right away. It makes me feel like you're really with me all the time—even in your sleep. I was never able to fall asleep in anybody's arms, just could never make it. But with you—with you I have such a good, protected feeling, I just pop off." She'd paused. "Mostly, I suppose it's that you make me feel like I want most to feel—like a woman. Oh, shit, I hope I don't sound cute or coy. But I mean it. I mean, it's a new feeling for me, never had it until you. I'm not a sexpot or a doormat and I know with you I never will be. It's like screwing. With you it's not screwing, it's just plain making love, being loved and loving. I don't know. Oh, God, Sheldon, you're going to be impossible to live with now. I've made you sound like a fucking paragon and I should have kept my big Texas mouth shut."

That same year he called her from New York a

week before Christmas: would she please meet him in Paris? They could celebrate the holidays at the Ritz.

No. She couldn't. And wouldn't. But why couldn't Sheldon come to Monte Carlo? She was having turkey dinner with all the fixings for all the lonely American orphans around here. One of her friends who had just flown in had concealed two packs of Pepperidge Farm Turkey Stuffing in his golf bag. Sheldon of course said he would be there and "What can I bring?"

"Just bring yourself. And keep your fly zipped up tight, you hear?"

By the summer of 1973 he had made the decision to revise his life. Drastically. If he could sell out his share of the company to Howard Mitchell. But it took an eternity, Howard being tough and hard-nosed about every picayune penny, every escutcheon on every drawer, before they could even reach a level of understanding and turn over the problems to the lawyers. Because Sheldon tended to be superstitious about premature announcements of his activities or plans, he never told Simona that he was definitely going to move to Monaco until he was totally positive he would be able to do it:

And when he did tell her, he made an occasion of it, a stellar evening. It was last year. He'd taken her to the concert, for this was the evening the Russian violoncellist Rostropovitch performed, with the orchestra being conducted by Khachaturian in his own compositions.

And there'd been the environment itself: the audience sitting in the 13th-century courtyard, with the two grand staircases curving down to hold the orchestra in their marble embrace. Directly behind him and Simona in a private box sat Prince Rainier, Princess Grace, and their children, while high above the palace the arching August sky was like a great tiara of stars.

Afterward he drove her to Le Pirate, where in the garden of this seaside restaurant they'd had a late supper, and where he made his announcement, the capping of this ritual night. . . .

The house now felt damp, chilly. "Would you like me to build a fire, Simona?"

Simona in the adjoining kitchen said yes, and how would he feel about a mushroom omelet and a salad complete with herbs from her garden? Then: "Did you say you would build a fire?"

"Yes."

"Oh, that would be lovely, and then we can do it on the rug in front of the fireplace. I can't wait."

After he'd stacked the small logs and kindling, he lit the crumpled papers beneath and it wasn't long before the blaze began to warm the white-walled room.

"Mygod, Sheldon, that's a talent I never suspected you had!"

"What's that?"

"Making a good fire."

"Every boy scout can."

"Don't tell me you were a boy scout. *You*, Sheldon?"

"Scout's honor."

"Where?"

"In Detroit. Troop 29. St. Paul's Cathedral."

"St. Paul's? Is that a Catholic or—"

"No, it's Episcopalian."

"Why, Sheldon—" She stepped out of the kitchen and put her arms around him. "How very chic of you."

More than chic. It was unprecedented.

Changed his entire life; it became his passport to a new universe.

It would never have happened had it not been for Andy Ward, the boy who sat next to him in math, Andrew Collingsworth Ward: Sam and Andy were bonded in friendship by their shared passion for stamp collecting. The two of them would spend hours after school negotiating trades, studying the Scott catalogue. He always went to Andy's house, not because it was near school but because it was on Boston Boulevard and in those days Boston Boulevard was considered the Park Avenue of Detroit, though he didn't know it; all he knew was that it was beautiful to look at, uncluttered and clean and it seemed like a thousand miles from his own neighborhood. . . .

No matter which way he looked at it, his view of

this particular Jewish community looked wrong, felt wrong to him. Like his feelings for his mother. He wanted to be THE American boy. But his mother with her German-Yiddish accent, her seeming lack of understanding of what he was or how he felt . . . frustrated him at every turn. And even though he loved her and thought he knew how much she loved him, there were these terrible contradictory forces that made him almost hate her at times; he couldn't help it, and he would hurt her feelings. And then would try to make up for it by a show of tenderness or helpfulness, and most of the time he failed. And one night he failed mortifyingly: It was during one of those party evenings, his mother having in several couples, "the girls" and their husbands, the women playing Mah Jongg, the men pinochle: a babble at the card tables or at the buffet where people kept returning and returning. . . .

And the way they looked: the women in dresses shiny as mirrors, their corsets pressing, squeezing their bosoms up into great balloons of flesh. . . .

"Samela—" his mother's voice reached out for him as he came through on his way to his room. "I was just telling the girls how nice you sound when you do your part." To the girls: "Such a fine voice he's got, how he speaks English!"

"Not now, Mom!" It was the school play, an amateur pageant called "Robin Hood." He was a troubador who read from a parchment scroll announcing the arrival of King Arthur.

"Mom, I—"

"Hey, come on, boychik, don't be so bashful already!" From Lennie Levine's father at the pinochle table.

"Samela, please. For your mother?"

"No—"

"All right. Not all of it, just do a little, it's so beautiful the way you do it. Come, boobela. For me."

For her. Yes. No. Oh God: and seeing her cheeks flushing pink with pride . . .

He was scared and he refused to show it; he was angry with her for forcing him into this, even granting she did it out of pride and, yes, love, and so he said all right he would do it.

Awkwardly, in pain, his heart pounding, he took his stance in front of the cabinet with the ruby-colored Bohemian glassware. . . .

"Shhh, everybody!" his mother warned.

Sammy swallowed, and began: "All ye merry gentlemen, stout citizenry all, our good master—"

But the eating, the smacking sounds of enjoyment went on in relentless counterpoint.

If this recital was so important to his mother or for her friends, why did they almost ignore him, humiliate him? Yet he wouldn't let her down . . . or himself. He had to try to go on:

" — our good master, the King is — " A spasm of coughing. "The King is — " But he'd choked on his own rage and misery and he couldn't understand why his mother couldn't understand what she was putting him through. . . .

No matter how much she loved him or how proud she wanted to be in front of her friends, how could she really love him and make him stand up here and make a stammering fool of himself . . . ?

"What is it, Samela?" His mother was half out of her chair.

He stared at her, he couldn't answer. He was too weak, almost faint; his throat was tight, he couldn't swallow. And what made it even worse was knowing he would be living this way for the rest of his life—or if he didn't, then what would he do, where in the world would he go?

His tears were sudden and he couldn't hold them back. And he ran blindly to his room. The crying wouldn't stop, nor would the sweating, the sudden weakness, the nausea — he stumbled into the bathroom and was sick. . . .

It didn't help. The taste in his mouth wouldn't go away. It stayed with him for days. And just when he would begin to forget about it, his mother—no doubt out of love, pride — would do something innocent, terrible, that would bring it all back again.

As for the Jewish girls his own age, well, in a way, being with them was like being with his mother: he was always torn between wanting and not wanting, between caring and not caring. If they were bright, they weren't very pretty; and if they were pretty, they weren't very bright. He always seemed to compare them with those gentile girls of his active imagination who were so relaxed, less nervous, less eager; he imagined that they were more polite, smarter: also harder to please, harder to kiss or touch:

All those hot, sweaty summer nights when he would lie in his bed trying to go to sleep and staying wide awake, a prisoner of his own confused desires: and if he didn't think of the Jewish girls he knew, he thought of their parents. Sure, he realized they were all nice to him, they were good people—yes, but if they were, then why did he keep having this awful feeling, as if he didn't belong with them? Didn't belong . . .

When he was thirteen, even then, he would make those secret little trips to certain parts of Detroit: he would go window shopping on Washington Boulevard where the smart specialty shops were and where he saw men and women who were driven by chauffeurs, where the boys wore the sort of clothes he really liked but couldn't afford, where he saw girls who all seemed slim, beautiful. (Lennie Levine called them *"shiksas,"* but the way he said it made it sound like an insult; he couldn't understand that.) Sometimes he would walk out along Jefferson Avenue, along the river, to get those fairytale views of the estates in Grosse Pointe, where gardeners tended the lawns and tipped their hats to the ladies of the house as they passed by. . . .

It was at Andy Ward's house that he got his first actual close-up of how "the other people" lived.

When he first went to Andy's house on patrician Boston Boulevard, the experience was a shock of joy: this house, which he would remember always, this house with its pale gray stone facade, its interior of dark paneling, fine old furniture, genuine antiques, and there was a billiard room. The Wards were one of the oldest families in the city, and though Mr. Ward was not much of a businessman and had dissipated his inheritance except for the house, he seemed to make up in elegance what he lacked in affluence. The door to that home was the heavenly portal. And when Sammy entered he even felt he was a different person. He was in awe of the serenity of that home. And in awe of Andy's father, whom he called "sir." One Monday night Sammy had dinner at the Wards'. The food, though first class, was spare. It was served on silver platters, not pushed at you: "Eat, Samela—eat, Boobela!"

And after dinner Andy took him along to his scout meeting which was held in the basement recreation room of St. Paul's Cathedral:

Sammy got his unforgettable view of Troop 29, the city's most elite troop.

When he compared the scouts from the Temple Beth Israel with these kids with their crisp uniforms, special sweaters, badges and red and black kerchiefs . . . well, you just couldn't!

This exposure made his own life even more untenable. Until the day Andy said, hell, if he wanted to join 29 maybe it could be done. One thing in

Sammy's favor was that Maynard Lanford, the young scoutmaster, was also an ardent stamp collector.

"I talked with the scoutmaster," Andy reported a week later, "and he said you could join our troop. If you got voted in."

Voted in. He didn't have to be very bright to know his chances. The day a Jew ever got into Troop 29 would be like the end of the entire world. But Andy said: "I know what you're worried about, but, well, you've met most of the guys and they all like you and nobody said anything about your—your not belonging to St. Paul's."

"Andy—if you're kidding me—"

There was little sleep for the rest of that week. Sammy would wake up in the middle of the night and to keep himself from thinking of the meeting and the vote scheduled for the following Monday night, he would turn on the study lamp on his desk and he would open his blue-bound Scott Stamp Album and he would try to lose himself, gazing at those exotic, blazing beauties from Mozambique and from Madagascar.

When the meeting took place, all went matter-of-factly: he and the other two candidates were asked to leave the room and to wait outside in the hall while the votes were taken. Half an hour later scoutmaster Lanford opened the door and asked only one of the other boys to come in, and he asked Sammy to come in:

And Sammy Bernstein became a tenderfoot with Troop 29 of St. Paul's Cathedral in Detroit.

And he passed his Second Class scout test and his First Class scout test, and the following summer he went to Troop 29's camp for four weeks; and if Sammy felt some of the boys were a bit chilly toward him, Maynard Lanford, the scoutmaster, made a point of being friendly. Lanford, tall, slim, blond, was a walking Arrow collar ad, right off the cover of the *Saturday Evening Post,* or more like the heroes of F. Scott Fitzgerald.

Until.

Until, at the end of his third week, Sammy awakened one night aware that someone was sitting on his tent cot. And then he felt something, a hand on his leg and touching his crotch: it was the hand of scoutmaster Maynard Lanford:

And that was why Sammy Bernstein never became an Episcopalian.

His being a member of Troop 29 tended to alienate him from most of the Jewish kids he knew. It also inspired dreams — maybe someday he would go to New York. Maybe someday he would . . .

But that was far off. That took money. Cutting grass in his neighborhood brought in fifty cents per lawn. And his part-time job at Sheim's Department Store found him in a cubicle, hot and sunny, in the back of the top floor amid high stacks of flat cardboards, each with the lavender logo of Sheim's—*Detroit's Finest*—and he would open the cardboards along the scored lines and fold them into boxes. This earned him twenty cents an hour. He had a helper, Marty Feinberg, pimpled and nervous, who would vanish into the toilet every day after lunch and masturbate.

When he confessed how he felt to Andy Ward, Andy suggested there might be a job as caddy where he was working for the summer, the Grosse Pointe Golf and Tennis Club (two elders of St. Paul's were on the Board of Governors). The following Sunday morning he went with Andy out to Grosse Pointe, right along the river, passing the Ford estate and the mansions of other members of the automotive aristocracy. When Andy introduced him to the pro, the man made a long and piercing survey of him. "What's your name?"

"Bernstein. Sam Bernstein."

The pro scratched his stalwart jaw. "You don't look it." Then: "Listen, kid, we can use you on Andy's sayso. But if you want to caddy here . . . well, let's see, how about we call you Bradley? Sam Bradley. Okay?"

What was in a name? Everything, apparently.

Imagine how Sammy felt when he heard himself addressed on the golf course:

"See you next Saturday, Bradley." ... "That's one ball you'll never find again Bradley." ... Before the summer was over he was caddying exclusively for a vice-president of General Motors, Sheldon Trowbridge. (Mr. Trowbridge was just like Mr. Ward, except that he was richer.) Sam noted the man's manners, his way of speaking with all that authority, his easy superior smile; his way of telling a dirty joke to another player but making it sound clever, funny, never offensive. Above all, there was his voice — modulated, never harsh, even when he muttered a curse over a bad putt.

Each Saturday and Sunday morning Trowbridge would greet him with that cordial voice, warm, yet somehow cool, so that you'd never misread him or think you were his best friend or anything. "Morning, Bradley, how are you?" (Unlike Lennie Levine's father, who ran into him one day outside the Book-Cadillac Hotel. Mr. Levine stopped him on the sidewalk and thrust out his arms, clamping his fingers over Sammy's cheeks and crying out: "Samela, boychik, so how's by you?")

At the end of the golf season, in his locker, there was a gift from Sheldon Trowbridge: a black leather wallet.

There was a name on it imprinted in small gold letters: S. Bradley. ...

Came the day to fill out the admission form for entrance to State University. The first line read:

"Your name. Please print." Sam Bernstein printed:

SHELDON BRADLEY

"My boy scout, lover—" Simona was ridding herself of her jeans.

The rain was unabated, still thudding on the tile roof. He and Simona on the thick Moroccan rug lay nude now in a dapple of firelight. . . .

Perfection.

But he couldn't quite respond, couldn't quite dispel those Detroit years . . .

He kissed her and his lips seemed numb with recollection.

Simona was stirring and then, "What is it, Sheldon?"

"Nothing. *Nothing.*" If he could only burn the memoirs of his youth!

"Look — why don't we — I mean, for now, why don't we have one of your lovely martinis."

Sheldon was relieved at once. Her quick perception was a blessing. He rose and tied his polo shirt around his middle and he heard Simona's soft laugh, her familiar testimonial to his "modesty." At the table on the other side of the room he set out two cocktail glasses, opened the Tanqueray gin.

"Another thing I adore about you, Sheldon, is that every guy over forty-five I know swears off martinis forever. But not you. You not only still drink them but you have them straight up with an olive. That's positively antediluvian and very refreshing. Hurry up. I can't wait."

He looked over at her. "You're the original Can't Wait girl, aren't you?"

"Now or never. That's me."

"Simona, the Now Girl."

She was standing by the fireplace, and he crossed the room and handed her the drink. And Detroit had totally receded. There was Athens now and there was that renewed pulsing in him. Simona reminded him of one of those eternal women, the figures he'd seen on the ancient Porch of Maidens across from the Acropolis. . . .

Before the drinks were finished he was holding her, and they were lying entwined on the rug again. There was no more numbness, and as he mouthed the hard crest of her breast, he felt her hand ever so lightly grazing his erection . . .

He always had to know more of her, he never seemed to be able to get the full, ultimate sensation of knowing all of her: he caressed her hard tender thigh, he caressed her vagina, tasting, tonguing her now, his sensibilities aroused by this tactile awareness of her deepest person. And then seeing her now, her head turned, as she bit her lips, as her pelvis began to rise, tremble.

It was just then as her body arched upward that he went inside her; and knowing she felt the throb of him, and then hearing her cry out:

Now.

Now. . . !

6

Now in tent 88: As in a Wagnerian opera, John McFarland entered just as there was a boom of thunder, a diamond slash of lightning above Mount Agel. An onslaught of rain. "Caught that call right on the button, lovie." He consulted his digital stainless steel watch.

"My husband"—Marie turned to Nick—"is in love with time."

"Got great news."

"Oh?" Nick saw her pale green eyes widen with interest. Marie, from any angle of vision, was a figure to admire, her titian hair scarfed, the rust-colored caftan slit along one side, exposing a long, slender thigh.

"Won't have to make that trip next Friday."

"You won't?" Relief marked her features. "That's the best news ever."

"Just talked to Willy. Won't have to make that African run after all."

"The last time he was in Africa, Nick," Marie revealed, "he was sound asleep in his hotel while fifteen people were shot to death right in the lobby."

"Sixteen," John corrected her.

"Every time I read about those people in the papers it's always what John calls a local scrap. But it always ends with a government shake-up and I don't know how many killed. Thank God you won't have to go back there."

"Right!" A pause. "They're coming here. To me. That is, the Deputy Defence Minister is."

Marie, in dismay: "I thought the deal was off."

"Come on, Marie, stop shooting blanks. This is the biggest deal I ever got close to, the biggest." McFarland seemed lit by some inner voltage. "Nick, my friend, let me tell you, and this is only between us, me lad. What I have coming up is pure gold. Potentially. And the guy who's arriving here to seal the deal is the brother of one of the biggest black leaders of one of the smallest countries in Africa. They're under an arms embargo and no one will do business with them. Except John McFarland. No one thinks they can get the stuff into that country, but I will."

"How will you work it, Johnny?" Nick was admittedly impressed with the sheer *chutzpa* of this improbable, wild, black-eyed New Jersey Irishman.

"How will it work? I'll stick my neck out is how. I'll work it the only way it ever works: juice, connections and leverage. Marie is worried because one of my men called especially to advise me against it. I fired him right then and there on the telephone because in my considered opinion he didn't know the difference between chicken shit and chicken salad."

"John—couldn't you say that in decent English—"

"Up the English!" McFarland jabbed his fisted forearm skyward.

"I don't like it, John. Maybe it's just a feeling. No, it's more than that. The odds are against you. Listen, John, you're not nineteen years old anymore, you don't have to prove anything to yourself anymore—"

"Lovie, you know damn well I couldn't sleep nights if the odds weren't against me." The arms broker in his khaki shorts and basketball shoes kept jutting out his mammoth hands. "Listen, Marie, if I pull this one off, you're going to be the richest girl in your own hometown. And don't you forget it."

"The richest widow."

To Nick: "Why is it women have such a nose for disaster?" Back to Marie: "The only buzz I ever get in this business nowadays is pulling off the impossible deal. So let's not give papa a rough time. Okay, lovie?"

"All right, John." Resignation. "When is this man due here?"

"July first. Mark it."

Nick watched Marie. She was cool. Yes. But loving.

She cared, she worried about McFarland just as—the
old pain came alive in him again—just as Jane used
to worry about him. Jane always anticipating or warning him if she thought he might run into possible
trouble. Not once since had there been a real woman
for him. His current girl was Eileen Blake. He had a
date to go to her place later, a matinée. But she was
no prize of femininity, not Eileen. She was Miss
Efficiency of 1975, secretary to the manager of the
brokerage firm of Grey, Young & Pierson — or, as
Nick referred to them: GYP.

No, it wasn't Eileen, it wasn't anyone. Not after
Jane. Why in Christ's name hadn't he gotten her out
of the States, why had he hung in there? And Jane,
and the child inside her—gone now. Why? Why?

"See you later." But before leaving, McFarland's
outsized hands enclosed Marie's breasts as he kissed
her. "The gun is the bride of war, and you're *my*
bride, lovie. And don't you ever forget it!"

"Nick—" Marie, offered him a Scotch on the rocks
as McFarland hurried out of the tent, back to the
apartment to get onto that telephone again — "what
happened to Sheldon? I went to his tent just before
lunch and he had gone."

"Last time I saw him, he and Simona were working
over a hot backgammon board."

"I'm giving a dinner party July fifth. I wanted to
invite him and Simona. And you."

"The fifth?" Nick tried the Scotch. "I don't know
about that, I might be too tired. That's the day after

the fourth. We're heading into our Bicentennial Year, Marie, and on July Fourth I'll be standing at attention all day saluting Old Glory—"

Marie's wry smile. "Yes, I can just picture you, Nick." Then: "Anyway, you won't forget. The fifth. Bring the lady of your choice."

"If any."

There was a moment, and then, as if needing to make small-talk, she asked if he'd had any luck finding an apartment for Sheldon.

Not yet.

Absently or perhaps not, she undid the scarf and exposed her long roseate hair. "He's quite a perfectionist, isn't he?"

"A super one, Marie."

"Do you think he and Simona will get married?"

Nick thought it more than possible.

"He's known her for a long time, hasn't he?" Again the apparently casual question seemed more than chitchat.

"Not really. They met back in 1970 but nothing happened until Sheldon started to summer here a few years ago. That's when they got together."

"He is—well, he doesn't talk much about himself."

Nick nodded. "The way I read Sheldon, he's had a lot of bad news in his life but he never bores anyone with it. He's one of those cats who lives strictly for the present. Or seems to."

Marie, with what could only be called the naiveté

of a local girl who has spent most of her life as a voyeur of the chic international league but who has never been part of it herself, pressed another question: Sheldon seemed to know so many important people; was it through his business? Or was it that he moved in the right circles?

"Both," Nick said. "He knows everyone, though you'll never hear him drop name one." Then: "You know, Marie, antique furniture has never sent me up. I guess I had too much around as a kid. Sheldon really has a feel for it, a love. After I met him at that dinner party in New York I kept running across stories about him. There was one in the *Times*. He put on an outstanding exhibit for the Metropolitan Museum. The big collectors respect Sheldon for his fantastic knowledge. And his integrity. He's a dude who does business with all of them—from the Rockefellers right down to the Rothschilds." Nick grinned. "Or should I say from the Rockefellers all the way up to the Rothschilds?"

Mirth touched the green eyes. Somewhat hesitatingly she said: "Don't you think Sheldon is too old for Simona? Though in his case one doesn't really think of age, I suppose." Nick noted her animation. She did seem to have some sort of fix on Sheldon. But what? Was it the distinct contrast between him and her husband? Was it possible that she'd never quite recovered from her father's premature death and Sheldon had become a sort of paternal symbol?

Or was this animation really more nervousness, her way of concealing her intuitive dread of the emissary from the Third World . . . ?

"I think I'll have a drink." Marie reached for the bottle of House of Lords.

"I've never seen you touch booze, Marie."

"Now you do, Nick." She contemplated the smoky amber liquid in her glass. A bleak and meditative interval. Then without warning, in a burst, as if to herself: "Oh God, I wish this summer were over!"

PART II *July*

*It was to be a summer long and sun-hazed; and often
when I looked up to the ocher-walled palace of
the Prince high on its rocky eminence it was veiled
in mist.*

*Golden mist hung over the airport of Nice, one of
the most intimate and welcoming airports I've ever
seen. That was the day John McFarland drove in to
meet the plane of the African Defence Minister,
whom he had first met six months ago in the man's
capital.*

*Adi Kuandi, as I remember, was not an imposing
figure, being short and stubby but with surprisingly
slender, graceful hands. The minute curls of his hair
lay matted like an ebony skullcap upon his head; the
wide mouth made a fleshy oval in his face. It was his
eyes, though, that held one, for they seemed at once*

101

on the edge of laughter and yet with a depth reflecting a terrifying shrewdness, a mirror of profound sorrows and the sense of survival.

The Defence Minister wore a lightweight suit of beige, neat and anonymous; his shoes, however, were of suede, made in Britain.

As they drove toward Monte Carlo along the sea, McFarland, being the solicitous host, announced that he'd engaged a limo with chauffeur for his guest's visit. And the first thing the man said, after conveying the cordial greetings of his Chief, was that he preferred to drive himself and that on these business missions he found relaxation at the wheel of a sports car: his smile suggested an awareness of this boyish and non-military indulgence. "You've got it. Consider it done, Mr. Minister."

Though Europe was not new to him, Monte Carlo was:

It was the season of the tourist, who was visible everywhere in the principality asserting his territorial prerogative; but this season there were not as many madras plaid jackets or rhinestone-framed sunglasses. However, there were now many more people from West Germany, their Mercedes' in an awesome cavalcade of affluence.

Monied Italians also raced in from the border in their Maseratis and lavished the liras from their bankrupt country upon the green baize tables of the Casino, while less privileged Italians arrived daily by bus for a day's excursion. The buses disgorged

*their greedy and naive passengers, who hurried into
the Café de Paris, for that is where most of the slot
machines were installed: this section of the Café de
Paris was a kind of Las Vegas in microcosm, with all
the silver shine of all the slots, all the tense, bent
figures tugging all the levers and believing they
could beat these machines with all the pre-adjusted
odds deadly fixed against the players. Yet it never
ceased: the mono-music of the slots now and then
broken by the brief cascade of coins or the rare flood
of francs signaling the jackpot's crescendo. By night-
fall the Italians climbed back into the buses to start
the hot ride back to their* patria pasta. . . .

*I remember on this evening, my good friend Nick, at
his station in the barroom confiding in me that he
had taken his first step for "an organization which
shall be nameless, called the IRS. Anyway, I've now
become a member of the Ignoble Order of Fink-
hood." But I must say this latest caper of his was
purest Harper Nicholson: for he had determined that
rather than* lead *the agency to tax defrauding
Americans, it would be more palatable for him to
mislead them. . . .*

*This was the same night I'd found myself at the
Summer Sporting Club among the denizens of the
high life who were dancing to the Brazilian beat or
jazzily coupled up doing the hustle: A great glinting
of emeralds and diamonds; a dazzle in the blue*

darkness beyond the roof which was rolled back to expose us to the lofty stars in their eternal beauty; and a splendid full moon, though its ancient mystery since that "first giant step for mankind" had been lost to me forever. (A different moon now than the one Caesar saw when he assembled his fleet in the harbor of Monte Carlo, preparing to do battle with Pompey.)

Several companions were on hand that night. Sheldon Bradley and Simona dining tête-à-tête to celebrate the end of the long negotiations with his partner, the transactions completed and the funds now in Monaco. But Sheldon had had to take a brutal beating on his capital gains at the hands of the IRS (not, mind you, that any of us had to weep in pity for him . . .).

A few tables away from Sheldon's were the McFarlands — John and Marie, entertaining their African guest, who was one of twenty-six very poor black children by his father's eighteenth wife, and who, now, at forty, was being addressed as "Mr. Minister."

7

"Mr. Minister—" John leaned forward in the black leather swivel chair at his desk — "to get to our inventory." He consulted his papers. "Let's see now if I have it correct." John sought verification on the number of MIG-21 fighter planes, the Russian AK automatic assault rifles, the RPG-7 rockets, the SA-7 missiles, ammunition and flamethrowers.

"Now about those MIG-21s, Mr. Minister. Yes, I can get them. The lowest price I can quote you is three-quarters of a million dollars per plane. But with your revised budget, I'd suggest you take the MIG-17 or MIG-19. Egypt is willing to unload its surplus. My man there has already inspected them and he tells me they're in excellent condition. They'll cost you about a hundred and fifty thousand dollars apiece fully equipped. Which means you can get a full

105

squadron, twelve of them, for the price of a couple of
MIG-21s. A better situation for you, Mr. Minister,
don't you agree?"

"I appreciate your concern, Mr. McFarland, but I'll
have to consult my brother before making a decision."

And you'd better decide to skip the MIG-21s, my
friend: Johnnyboy doesn't have the kind of cash it
takes to pick up aircraft like that. In that bracket you
need the backing of the CIA or a biggie like Sam
Cummings. But, on the other hand, Cummings was
much too legitimate to deal with the likes of Kuandi.
And didn't they all know it? Right!

"Now, sir," John continued, "as for the ten
thousand AKs, no problem. They're already confirmed. Ready for crating. At two hundred dollars
apiece." McFarland's man in Libya had put him onto
the whole lot there at forty dollars apiece. Russia'd
been flooding that country with AKs. And all John
had to do was get them out of there. Against regula-
tions. But those boys bribed easy. They had swivel
heads that turned to the tune of the buck.

"Two hundred dollars seems steep for the AKs, Mr.
McFarland. Considering the volume we need."

"Mr. Minister, no one will sell those rifles to your
country. I have to use very special means to obtain
them under cover for you." On these AKs Johnnyboy
wasn't about to hand out bargains. He knew Kuandi
needed them. And Kuandi knew goddam well the
risks he, McFarland, would be taking to deliver

them. Without waiting for the Minister's answer, he continued: "Now about the bazookas, Mr. Minister. You don't want anything that obsolete. I can get you the RPG-7. It's the best weapon today. Individually launched rocket. They'll cost you a hundred and fifty thousand dollars apiece complete. These RPGs can even knock out a train."

"What is the price of the extra rocket for these RPG-7s?"

"A drop in the bucket, sir. Merely fifty dollars a drop."

The Minister had been sitting there marking down all prices, doing his computations. If McFarland's figures were correct, and they were, this gentleman so far had spent a little over four million dollars. More to come.

"Now to the Holy Grails, Mr. Minister—"

Kuandi looked up. "I beg your pardon, sir?"

"That's what we call the SA-7s in America. The Russians call them Strealas. A first-rate portable missile, as you know. First rate. I've seen them in action. They drop low-flying planes like ducks. You'll need a minimum of five hundred to start with. Correct, sir?"

"Yes, that was our estimate. And the price, Mr. McFarland?" The Minister, his gold pencil at the ready, looked at him.

"Five hundred dollars apiece. Brand new, that is." McFarland watched the man jot down the figures. Keep going, my friend, there's a good chap. Add another two hundred and fifty thousand dollars to the contract. This lot only cost me twenty thousand bucks. But who takes all the risks? Johnnyboy.

The flamethrowers next. Fifty of them, at five hundred each.

As Kuandi was doing his arithmetic, John poured more coffee. Marie had sent the maid in with the silver tray. Marie had lowered her aim, changed her stance; at least she seemed to have lost some of her stupid fears:

At the Summer Sporting Club last night she had gotten a close-up of the Defence Minister, and she no longer had her ass in an uproar about all the dangers this deal might bring:

She felt easier now that she'd talked to him, had learned more about the man — that he came from a very small village, had been educated in a Catholic missionary school, that he had been selected to attend Magdalene College at Oxford. How disorienting it had been for him to return to Africa, to resume tribal customs, to marry an uneducated girl from his village. How insecure and confused he'd felt, split between two cultures, trying to cope with the two worlds he lived in:

And it wasn't until his brother came to power that Adi Kuandi began to feel at home in his skin once again. Marie was touched by the Minister's struggles, his life, his new image of himself, his new swagger of arrogance; even his boyish fascination with Monte Carlo. . . .

The Minister crossed his legs and studied his splendid suede shoes. "Have you been able to locate any Welrods for us, Mr. McFarland?"

"No sir. They're out. Collector's item. As you probably know, they were made by Enfield in England during World War II. Can't pick them up anywhere. What I suggest is the Czech Scorpion. The finest silencer pistol around. And I can deliver them to you for one hundred and forty dollars apiece. Okay, sir?"

"Two hundred of them will suffice." When it came to numbers and costs, the Minister's diction was very crisp, very fucking goddam crisp. But he knew that without Johnnyboy, his country couldn't even import a BB gun.

"Okay, sir. Now to the routing. What I'd appreciate from you, Mr. Minister, is information on any possible detour points in case of unexpected emergencies or in case of—"

Kuandi interrupted. "Mr. McFarland—" The stocky little man lit up a cigar. "Mr. McFarland, you must know that we have no one we can depend or rely on, only a few trustworthy people. The ones your agents are in touch with. We—in Africa—we are living in great confusion. There is so much division. Governments fall overnight. My country, like all the others, is presently interested only in self-survival."

And speaking of self-survival, you sonofabitch, you're also interested in that fifteen percent kickback you hope to get from one John McFarland. . . .

"Speaking of self-survival, Mr. Minister, I've been thinking about your appropriations"—and my limited cash— "and I really must discourage you on those MIG-21s. That model couldn't make it to your country from Egypt without a fuel stop, say in Khartoum. And you know that's definitely out. Whereas the MIG-17 and 19 we can disassemble and load one by one onto C-130s. The C-130 can make it nonstop. No refueling necessary. All we'd need is an overflight permission from Sudan."

"I fear we shan't be able to get that permission."

"Then we'll have to go out to sea. Over the Indian Ocean and come in that way." Jesus, McFarland pondered the risk: via the sea route he could never get those planes and cargo insured. One C-130 with one MIG-17 aboard crashing into the sea and he'd be out—better not try tallying up a loss like that now. . . .

That damn cigar. John slid back one of the glass doors. At once a sea breeze ruffled the map, blew up one corner. John reached for the pistol on the side of his desk and weighted down the map.

The Minister, he had observed, admired this weapon; he had been eyeing it ever since the conference began at ten this morning. John decided this was the moment to give him the McFarland Gift Special. From his desk drawer he brought forth a black case and handed it to the Minister. Inside was the same pistol except this one was gold-plated and bore the initials "A.K."

The man's eyes dilated with pleasure. He fingered

the pistol, but with careful, understated gratitude he said: "How very kind of you, Mr. McFarland."

Fucking right he was kind: add to this pistol that silver Porsche he had rented for the Minister, and the underwriting of any Casino losses he might incur, as well as footing the tab for his hotel. And, just to round it all off, he would be asking Nick to arrange for some pussy, something that also took hard cash, nothing you could use your American Express or Diners Club card for.

All right. The horseshit was over. Now into the rest of the package. John only hoped that all his homework added up.

"First, the markings of the crates, Mr. Minister. Some will come through as 'Medical Supplies' and some as 'Farm Machinery.' No 'Automobile Parts,' that's out. I've had too much trouble with that phony label. And we brand our crates."

"Brand?"

"Yes, brand. Costs more but holds up. On your continent we worry about the heavy rainfall. Same as in Spain. I learned the hard way, Mr. Minister." And John recounted grimly how years ago he had brought a shipment of arms by plane from Panama and during the refueling stop in Barcelona the weather had turned against him, forcing a layover: there had been a night-long torrential rain, and the fake insignias and identification markings on the fuselage of the plane had been washed out, leaving the real insignias of the plane's origin embarrassingly visible.

The Minister seemed impressed and relieved. In

discussing the problems of routing the shipment, Kuandi said: "Our greatest concern—I mean to say, our greatest threat — as you know, comes from Uganda, from General Amin's military. Also, General Amin has trained and instructed his border tribes to keep our activities under constant surveillance. In other words, Mr. McFarland, no shipment will reach us unless every possible margin for error—"

"Yes, I know. 'When the bulls stumble, the butchers sharpen their knives.'" He quoted the old County Antrim axiom of his father. "But I think I've put together a workable solution."

The intercom buzzed. It was Marie: what were his plans for lunch?

"Anything that comes into that rosy-haired head of yours," John answered with characteristic flamboyance, but also for the Minister's benefit.

But when Marie suggested a formal lunch in the dining room or perhaps on the terrace, he immediately vetoed it; he didn't want to break the rhythm of this meeting: have the maid bring in a working lunch. After he hung up he said to Kuandi: "I hope you don't mind lunching American style, Mr. Minister. But our schedule—"

"Not at all. Delighted."

John unfolded the entire map and turned it around so that the Minister could follow the program.

"We'll ship the crates from this point—" he indicated an area in Czechoslovakia. "The ship—a thousand-ton coaster—gets loaded at this point." Loaded, my friend, at a cost to McFarland of one thousand bucks a day. But at least on this run he would be covered by Lloyd's. "No problems. Not yet. We sail down the Danube and into Varna in Bulgaria. And here's our first crossroad. Here we're given two choices. If we get Egypt's permission to unload the coaster in Alexandria or Port Said, transfer onto trucks and then load the crates directly onto the C-130s with the MIGs, we're all set to take off. I assume they'll give us that permission since we're buying the MIGs from them. But these days who can count on anything?"

"Unfortunately—"

"Okay. If Egypt plays tough, we have the second choice: we ship all the way straight through to Dar es Salaam—" which is Arab-cute for *Haven of Peace*. "But frankly, Mr. Minister, we'd rather avoid that. The East African coast is not very hospitable to shipping, as you know. Those high tides are rough, always give us trouble. At any rate, in Dar es Salaam we transfer onto trucks for the home stretch. And given a bit of Irish luck, Mr. Minister, your country will have its defensive arsenal." As for one John McFarland, this would be his magic mountain, a beautiful green mountain of money, enough to retire on. And make his grand woman of a wife happy forever and a day and a night.

McFarland went over to the built-in refrigerator, took out a bottle of Dom Perignon, popped the cork and poured two glasses. "Mr. Minister, shall we drink to this?"

He offered a toast to Kuandi and his big brother.

But now to the money.

Money?

Yes, money. Best discussed over champagne, right?

Right.

Payment by certified check?

Right!

Delivered by whom?

The Defence Minister in person.

Right.

In Monte Carlo or Geneva?

"I would prefer Monte Carlo, Mr. McFarland. I've grown very fond of this place and wouldn't mind getting a few more rounds at the gaming tables."

Right.

"The choice of currency is yours, Mr. McFarland."

"French francs are easiest to clear through the local bank, Mr. Minister."

"I am not certain about French francs. But in U.S. dollars this payment would not create any difficulties for my country, Mr. McFarland."

"Okay with me. I accept U.S. dollars any day. Only problem here is that it will take a day or two to clear the check with the Banque de France in Paris."

The Minister cleared his throat. But he didn't speak. He was contemplating his suede shoes again. McFarland wished to hell he could figure out what those fucking shoes meant to him. All he got now was silence.

"Anything wrong, Mr. Minister?"

"No. I was only wondering—that is, you see my own personal account is in a Geneva bank and—"

And you're only wondering how you're going to get your fifteen percent. Right?

"No problem, Mr. Minister. We'll plan on transferring your—ah—commission to Geneva."

"In Swiss francs." The Minister's instructions were hard and clear as diamonds.

"Right, sir." And may the good Lord bring you back to Monte Carlo in your good brown suede shoes and with your good certified check in your good black fist.

And then if war should come to Kuandi's land, Johnnyboy would get himself yet another big order:

There was a common adage among arms traders; it might have originated with Sam Cummings: "No matter who wins, we win; no matter who loses, we win."

8

"Nicky, me friend" — it was John McFarland tele-
phoning him at the bar of the hotel—"could you be
helping me? A little matter of sex for me African
paddy." McFarland went on in that Irish vaudeville
brogue he invoked when he was in a particularly
expansive mood. "Want a surprise package, me boy,
by midnight. Blond and blue-eyed, skin like milk."

Yes, Nick would oblige. He could arrange it even
though this chauvinistic procurement on behalf of
the Defence Minister went decidedly against his
grain.

A single phone call: coming up: one milk-skinned
object.

Time marched backward.

But when he left his office, the bar of the Hotel de
Paris, and crossed over to the Café de Paris for a

sandwich, the first person he saw was Janet Babcock, wife of the good Cincinnati dentist: Janet at a terrace table writing postcards.

Janet, looking up, was conspicuously pleased to see him. Clearly she was still a "Casino widow."

Wouldn't she like to take a look at some charming bits of real estate?

What sort?

Apartments.

For vacations?

Yes. And for income renting.

Speaking for Harry, her husband: no. Speaking for herself: yes.

Agreed.

It was apt to be one of those good days. His left palm sometimes told him. Gallantly he paid for Janet's coffee and with the change went through one of his rituals of superstition: he stepped into the gaudy arena of slot machines, selected one, played a single franc (about twenty-five cents) and clanked himself into some ripe fruit that dropped a handful of coins. Yes, definitely this augured well. He blew his profits on four packs of American cigarettes.

Janet apologized as she accompanied him to the TR 3: was she taking his time up? After all she was in no position to buy or even rent property this year. She didn't want to infringe on his day.

No problem, no sweat.

He'd already put in a good day's work. In the early morning hours he had driven up to the Monaco cemetery. At the eastern section, where foreigners were buried, he'd found his way to the tombstone of a Chicagoan whose demise he had recently read about. He had recorded the name and other facts carved in the marble slab and had returned to the M.C. library for a back copy of the local paper to check out the dead man's obit for his last known M.C. address. He would preserve this data until he had a few more non-leads to dispatch to the designated department of the IRS in Washington (who had agreed on a final seven hundred fifty dollars a month for his services).

Add to this positive beginning the commission he had received last week for a three-year rental-lease for an American refugee who had fled London's frosty tax climate, plus the sale of a small cottage outside Menton (a minute compensation for the total disaster the day he had taken Frederico and Alma A up into the hills to view that handsome contemporary villa: no way, Alma had stated. She had spent the first years of her marriage in the Connecticut countryside and the poison ivy, the mosquitos and solitude drove her bananas!)

In the TR 3, top down, Nick drove Janet along the water's edge, pointing out to her the new condos rising between the Loew's Monte Carlo Hotel and the Holiday Inn. He took her into the highrises to inspect apartments, to terraces with views of the Mediterranean that were aphrodisiacal:

Janet—oh, how she was digging it, already into it.

Her Cincinnati life, she exclaimed as her gaze moved across the coves and curves of the coastline, that life back home seemed hopelessly bleak, and how to face it again seemed impossible to imagine. . . .

To help her cope, Nick then showed her one more apartment—his own. Which, though modest, was on a very picturesque little street up on The Rock and just an Instamatic Kodak's click away from the palace of Her Serene Highness.

Half an hour later, in the bed which a few days ago had been warmed by cool Eileen Blake of GYP, Janet Babcock was nude in his arms, this Cincinnati Circe unhappy in the life she had made and regretted and from which she seemed fated not to escape: each year, she told him, it was another event in house-holding that gave her already stale "marriage a false illusion of contentment: a new kitchen, a new bar-becue patio, a new swimming pool and, last year, the conversion of the study into a projection room for those Saturday night porno screenings. . . .

Despite that most recent of refinements, she had to confess that she hadn't had an orgasm like this in she didn't know how long: "And you know, Nick"—she was stroking his thick, fair hair—"honestly, Nick, it's so wonderful to make love without having to watch a movie!"

When he and Janet left the apartment and started down the stairway he heard his telephone, turned and hurried back up to unlock his door, getting inside just in time to hear the last ring.

But as soon as they entered the bar of the Hotel de Paris, the bartender gave him a message: call Mr. McFarland. And while Janet went to the reception desk to check if her husband had returned, Nick telephoned the arms dealer.

"Nick—an emergency. We're in trouble. You know that girl you set up for my friend here?"

"Yes, the finest your money can buy." No understatement this—for there was no prostitution in Monaco, no whores on the pavements. Discretion was the order of the day; and elegance was the order of the nighttime *femmes de plaisir.*

"She showed up and he threw her out. He wants a chocolate drop." McFarland's voice was rough with impatience and puzzlement. "Can you imagine that paddy not wanting any of that choice blond pussy?" Could Nick now arrange for a black girl?

Yes, but it meant going to Nice. But he was going to Nice anyway: "I want to see about how I can get rid of this passport. The time is upon me. So I'll also do what I can to make this African cat of yours happy. I'm only doing it, Johnny, because I'm counting on you as a solid citizen around here to vouch for me with the good folks up on The Rock."

"Consider it done," McFarland assured him: Though his business operations might not have met the noblest ethics of commerce and though he most definitely did not travel in Rainier's circle, he was nevertheless considered in Monaco as a man who had contributed considerably to the principality's welfare; he had clout, not only because his wife was a Monégasque whose family was involved in civic functions, but also because he had been extremely generous in his donations to charities: the Red Cross, the hospital, the schools. . . .

When Janet Babcock returned, Nick ordered champagne, nothing less. They settled at one of the tables near the bar. And Janet reread a telegram that had been waiting for her at the front desk. "It's from my sister. Marion. She's the younger one. The one with all the brains in the family. She's going to join us here — it's her first vacation in three years." A pause. "I'm afraid she'll hate this place, it's everything she can't stand. But—"

"Well, then"—Nick grinned—"here's to your sister."

"Hi, there, Nicholson." It was the good dentist Babcock, his complexion showing the sunless pallor of a passionate Casino habitué. "Well, what's new?" To his wife: "And what have you been up to this afternoon, honey?"

In Nice, after having attended to the request of John McFarland, Nick made his historical visit to the United States Consulate. He told the consul, a woman of middle years, tall and sober-eyed and in command of an admirable objectivity, that he wished to obtain all the detailed information on renunciation of U.S. citizenship.

The consul nodded. No questions. Not yet. She provided him with three documents, which he could take home to study, though he scanned them immediately:

1. CERTIFICATE OF LOSS OF NATIONALITY OF THE UNITED STATES:
   (Prescribed by the Secretary of State pursuant to Section 501 of the Act of October 14, 1940 and Section 358 of the Act of June 27, 1952.)
2. STATEMENT OF UNDERSTANDING.
   (I, John Doe, understand that: I have a right to renounce my United States citizenship and I have voluntarily decided to exercise that right. Upon renouncing my citizenship I will become an alien in relation to the United States of America. . . .
3. OATH OF RENUNCIATION OF THE NATIONALITY OF THE UNITED STATES.
   (As provided by the Immigration and Nationality Act and pursuant thereto I hereby absolutely and entirely renounce my nationality in the United States and all rights and privileges thereunto pertaining and abjure all allegiance and fidelity to the United States of America. . . .

The consul patiently summed up for him, for his complete understanding, what this action meant, the precise nature of the privileges he would lose, the precise nature of his future status. She also informed him that he would have to show proof that he would obtain citizenship status in another country:

And finally she warned him that this act would be irrevocable. Then, after a rather long and searching look at him: "I hope you're not seeking this information for your own personal use, Mr. Nicholson."

Unprepared for this and for an instant unsettled by her question, Nick turned away from the consul's penetrating gaze. His eyes came to rest on the wall photograph of President Ford (the last time he had been here it had been Nixon who had smiled down on him).

"Is this intended for you personally, Mr. Nicholson?" the consul repeated.

"Yes. Why?"

"No reason. Except—well, it's simply that you look so—how shall I put it—so very American." A pause. Briskly then: "If you do decide to go through with this—and I have to remind you once more that it will be irrevocable—do you have any idea when you plan to do this?"

"I'm in no hurry. Sometime next week, maybe. In any case, in time to celebrate the Bicentennial."

The consul indulged him with a tepid smile. He saw that she was suddenly a bit, the merest bit, uneasy. He decided that instead of allaying her apprehensions with a bitter and painful account of the murder of his wife and unborn child or with his long list of grievances against the history of recent-day

America—he decided it might be more fitting to tell her the documented fact that the Nicholsons went back not only to the American revolution but that several of his antecedents were high ranking officers and that one of them, Hiram Nicholson, was General Washington's legal counsel and a close aide: "When they died they must have rested in peace," Nick told the earnest lady, "but today they must be spinning in their graves. . . . "

He had warmed the atmosphere and they could talk less formally. "We haven't had many of these requests, but I must say, Mr. Nicholson, with your background—I'm perplexed."

"So am I sometimes. Let's just call it a love/hate relationship." Nick pondered this glib statement and added: "No—it's probably a case of too much love."

She frowned. Was she regarding him as a freak? To make her feel better, or to establish another sort of hereditary link between past and present, he gave her a true account of his grandfather, who was dismissed from the Harvard faculty for bathing naked in the Charles River and then sprinting along the banks to dry off. "You might say," concluded Nick, "that Professor Nicholson was the first one to get into streaking."

It had to be said of this United States Consul that she performed her duties in good faith, for when she shook hands with Nick he got the definite vibration that she attempted with their parting handshake to imprint on his palm the Stars and Stripes forever.

9

For Marie, the early stages of her dinner party seemed too perfect to be true. As was the weather. From the terrace of the thirtieth floor, Monte Carlo and the great bend of the shoreline shimmered gold and mauve in the languishing twilight:

Too perfect. With John going out of his way to make this a felicitous occasion.

No vulgar jokes.

No terrifying tantrums.

No sudden rudeness.

Mentally she crossed herself. This occasion, which had had to be postponed until tonight, would, hopefully, be that much needed respite for both her and John. Adi Kuandi was gone, though he would be returning some weeks hence; but during his stay she had recognized certain plainclothesmen from her

brother's office (the Deuxième Bureau) hovering
around the building from time to time; also, the
Defence Minister had left behind, for John to pay,
Casino chits amounting to more than three thousand
dollars and an eight-hundred-dollar hotel bill.

But Marie fervently hoped that the effort and anxiety she'd put into this evening wouldn't show; her
dark red hair, after two hours at the coiffeur's, should
look quite perfect and she felt secure in this grand
living room with its satin and velvet chairs (John
insisted on reproductions because "they're sturdier
than those creaky antiques that'll split right from
under you and a person can fall and break his stupid
ass!").

A covert wish rose in her: if her father could have
lived to see her tonight so handsomely established.

Sheldon Bradley on the brocade divan near her,
with Simona at his side: It was a kind of social
feather in Marie's cap, having a man like him on
hand. She had seen him just the other evening in the
glass-walled dining room atop the Hotel de Paris (her
second cousin Jacques worked there as pastry chef)
and at his table were Sir Maxwell and Lady Epworth
and the American art collector, Mrs. Louise Smith-
son. . . .

Sheldon, if she allowed herself to admit it, did
bring out the best in her, she seemed to function so
beautifully in his company. Above all else it was his
eyes that held a particular interest for her: the gray

eyes, so reserved, and the way they seemed to tell or
see so much and yet never quite reveal his feelings:

As compared with John, whose dark eyes were
flash-like electric signs, making too obvious what his
mood was. She did love him. Though that love had
lost some of its luster. No woman could take his ways
year after year, his unpredictable turns that within
seconds could go from the most delightful nonsense
to the wildest fury; or the way at times he could
become almost poetic and at other times relentlessly
vulgar. . . .

Yet now, how everyone seemed charmed by him,
just as she had been at first: dazzled by his force, his
vitality. Now as he stood there in front of the rose
marble fireplace (fake, but he had insisted he had to
have it), he did command attention. No doubt of it.
And he made up with that drive of his for whatever
else he lacked; he may not have been as attractive as
Sheldon or Nick or Alma Ainsworth's friend, Frederico, but he was compelling with those black eyes
and the black hair and that inconsistent rosy,
cherubic face; he also looked quite dashing in the St.
Laurent safari suit, the Gucci belt and shoes.

"Well now"—inevitably after a few drinks, off
came the jacket, party or no party; John's eyes glim-
mered mischievously: he was in full form and the
Irish tones of his father were zealously replayed—
"now let me tell you one of me dad's favorite stories.
It's old as Paddy's potato field, but let me tell it—"

Marie stiffened.

"Don't worry, sweetlove, it's a respectable old wheeze." He put his glass on the mantelpiece and cleared his throat. "Seems me dad's best friend, Paddy Terrigan, was on his dyin bed and me dad says to him, 'Is there anything you'd want me to be doin for you?'

" 'Yes,' says old Paddy, 'would ye, once a year, on the anniversary of me death, get a bottle of the finest Irish whiskey and pour it over me grave?'

" 'Yes, me friend,' answered me dad, 'but would ye mind terribly if I passed it through me kidneys first?' "

Marie was relieved: enough laughter or titters to go around.

As John resumed his bartending, Nick's date, Janet Babcock, who was staying on in Monte Carlo awaiting her sister, turned to Marie: "You're lucky. You ought to hear the jokes my husband gets off back in Cincinnati. Talk about rough." Her candid American smile was a bit strained.

John handed Sheldon a martini refill.

"Easy, John." Sheldon raised a hand in protest.

"Never mind that, Sheldon. I'm host here. I'm boss."

Marie nodded. "His brothers," she told the group, "call him head of the Green Mafia."

As conversation resumed, Marie noticed the way Sheldon was studying the cabinet and she decided to ask him what she'd been wanting to ask him for some time. "Tell me, Sheldon, what do you think of that piece? From the way you're looking at it, I—"

"Let me put it this way." Sheldon spoke softly. "It's an antique, yes. The only thing is, it's a marriage. The top and the bottom are each perfectly legitimate except that they come from different families. And then some devious dealer introduced them and it was love at first sight."

"All right." John chuckled. "Well put, well put, goddamit. I'll buy it."

"You already have, John," Sheldon answered, and turned to light Marie's cigarette for her.

She was not displeased by the attention Sheldon was giving her. It made her wonder if anything was wrong between him and Simona. They were definitely not as warmly harmonious tonight as they customarily were.

From behind her chair she heard fragments of talk between Frederico and Nick:

"Listen, Nick," the young Italian was saying, "this Ferrari I told you about, it's a 1971 Dino, red, and not a hell of a lot of mileage. Through this friend of mine I can drive it away for about twelve thousand—"

"Twelve grand for a Ferrari?" Nick said. "Isn't that pretty cheap? Are you sure this car isn't hot?"

"That's not my problem, Nick. You know my problem. Listen, I've had a hard-on for that model ever since I saw the first one in New York. Nick, we've got to come up with something—"

"*You've* got to come up with something, Frederico."

"Yeah. I know."

The voices were low, conspiratorial. But none of this was Marie's business. There was a time when

Marie would have disapproved of Alma A associating
with a type like Frederico, but today she was a lot
more tolerant or sophisticated than in the days of her
youth: the loving Catholic girl with a strict but loving
father.

Yet he was the one who had sent her to London
after she had graduated from the lycée in Monaco; he
had paid for her year of English business school. And
when she returned to M.C. her bilingual abilities
won her jobs at once: she worked for American Express, and in the Yves St. Laurent boutique; she was
private secretary and business manager for the Greek
artist who painted portraits in the lobby of the Hotel
de Paris; and lastly she was given the responsible
position with Monte Carlo Business Services. . . .

And wasn't it this that had brought her to John
McFarland's attention, her having had to deliver the
telex to him. . . .

Oh, if her father were alive! If only he could see
how she was living now; he had died of a stroke just
a month before she had met John. How he used to
worry about her, just like her brother Claude at the
Deuxième Bureau and her uncle at the Casino—all
of them concerned that at twenty-five she was not yet
married. While all the girls, friends and relatives
she'd grown up with in Monaco were wives and
mothers. . . .

But she had had her day: a bride waiting before the
altar in St. Martin's church, standing there with her
brother, as John McFarland . . . "the strange, rich

American" . . . walked out of the vestry to come to
her side (whiskey and love on his tongue); and she
never dreamed she would be presiding at dinner
parties like this one high up in the Residence du
Parc. . . .

"—the gala, Marie—?" Alma Ainsworth was ad-
dressing her.

"What?"

"Princess Grace's Red Cross gala. Are you going?"

"We always have."

"Not this year," John interceded. "Your husband is
going to be in Prague and the Lord knows what other
Eastern Disneylands. But you'll be going, Marie.
Why don't you go with Alma? When it comes to
charity, you know where I stand."

"I like charity," came Frederico's unsolicited statement.

Marie was watching Sheldon again: he seemed
distracted or preoccupied this evening, even more so
now as he moved off without a word and stepped out
onto the terrace.

"Speaking of charity" — Frederico sauntered over
and sat down beside Simona — "you know something? Why don't you make me one of those belts
like the one you've got on, Simona. Only for me I'd
wear it around my neck."

"Any time, Frederico. It's easy. All you have to do
is place an order with me," Simona answered.

" 'Scuse me," Frederico was back on his feet.
"Want to change that tape."

Simona inhaled deeply from her cigarette and smoke grayed her fair features: it was plain to see why Sheldon was infatuated with her. She didn't seem to try for any effect. Her black dress was long, simple, elegant, a natural background for the modern design of her hand-crafted gold-link belt, with the now familiar old-fashioned gold watch hanging from it. Her grandfather, she once told Marie, had brought it from Kentucky to Texas in 1910.

Frederico began to dance. Not with Alma, who was sitting slightly slumped in the imitation Louis XV armchair, her eyelids drooping. No, it was Janet Babcock he was holding, and as they danced nearby, Marie heard him say: "Your husband, a dentist in Cincinnati? Have I got that right, Janet?"

"Yes."

"In Cincinnati—you mean like now?"

"He arrives back there tonight."

"Mrs. Babcock — Janet — what I want to know is like what can I do to make your stay enjoyable?"

"I'll tell you what you can do, Frederico, me lad, you can let a good man like John McFarland take over here." John, who seldom danced, had replaced the Italian, and though he was clumsy, was having a grand time; his spirits were infectious; and then Nick came over and, bowing with mock formality, asked Marie to dance.

Yes, this party was surely going to be a lively one, her best ever.

Until the telephone call.

It came shortly after dinner, which had been received with appreciative zest. Marie was not a gifted
cook, but between the two women in the kitchen —
one of whom used to cook and serve in her father's
house after her mother had died — the results could
always be depended upon.

When the telephone rang, most of the guests were
taking demitasse in the living room, though Sheldon
and Simona had gone out to the terrace.

Politely John excused himself to take the call in his
office. But after a while, an interminable time, Marie
began to grow nervous. This call — it could have
meant anything. Good or bad. Though she sensed
that whatever was going on was not good.

Finally she left the living room and hurried down
the hall to the eastern corner of the apartment where
John's office was located. The door was ajar.

Her fears were immediately confirmed. He was
still talking on the phone and from the way he kept
fussing with that pistol — the automatic Mauser (always loaded but with the safety on) which he used as
a paperweight—and his voice, furry, blocked, choked
with rage — Marie knew this voice. She was always
terrified by it.

A second telephone call. He pressed a lever of the
scramble box. He lifted the other receiver and after a
moment harshly shouted: "Hold on, Kevin, hold on!"

His brother.

Back to the first phone, and soon Marie heard
enough to know he was speaking with his lawyer in

Washington. When it was over he slammed down the instrument and got on to his brother. He and Kevin were very close, in touch with each other at least once a week. Kevin in Los Angeles was, like John, a high flyer, a big talker, a big manipulator. He happened to be in the movie industry, very much on the rise as a film distributor, with business operations in the U.S.A. and Montreal and Iran. . . .

"Kevin, you want to hear something, you want to hear the tough shit of all time? I just got the word from Wardell in Washington, sonofabitch tells me, after all those legal fees he's hooked me for, he tells me, this fucker tells me I've lost my appeal! The decision of the lower court has been sustained. No reversal! I've got to liquidate the Canadian—

"What? I'll tell you what: about a million six, or if I'm lucky and the IRS makes a deal with me, we might shave it to a million more or less — yeah, I know it was in the cards but—listen, Kev—how are you fixed out there? I need five hundred thousand minimum. Now. Tonight. No later than the first of the week—I need it because I'm due in Czechoslovakia and I can't do business, you understand, Kev — no cash, no deposit, no guns! It's for the first shipment with option money for the second round. But this deal, if I can pull it, is my biggest. It's tilt. You know what I mean—

"You what? Since when?

"Oh, for christsakes, you didn't tie up that much, did you? Why? Never mind. What the fuck good is that when the banks blank me as far as this deal is concerned. This deal is not even supposed to exist, I can't show my stupid Irish face in any fucking bank. But I thought I could at least count on you—

"Hey, hold it, Kev—something, something comes to me. That situation with the kid who worked for you. Yeah, last January; that mixed-up kid you said was trying to screw you. What's the status on that case?"

John had turned and seen Marie: "Goddamit, Marie—get out, get the hell out of here . . . !"

Marie felt the weakness in her knees and her throat was pulsing. She moved quickly, needing to gain control, poise, before facing her friends, before facing what was left of the evening:

But in less than a minute, as she was about to offer more coffee to her guests, John reappeared: or rather, he charged into the living room. He was almost unrecognizable. The rosy face was purple-dark, the veins at his temple were distended: "Jesusgod, holy mother Mary, how can those people do this to me!" He flailed his arms, he was still clutching the pistol.

No one was prepared, no one moved, frozen there in bewilderment, in an inertia of shock.

But his apparent lunacy, insanity, only seemed to be gathering more force: he kicked the first chair in his path and it crashed against the grand piano (which had never been played).

"John—" But Marie was as impotent as the others, and she knew there was no way to save or preserve the evening and her friends all knew it too.

In mortification she moved to the door with them as they took their leave in a storm of muttered embarrassments.

"John — " She attempted to stop him. He was charging toward the terrace.

Sheldon Bradley and Simona were still there. And they were startled by the sight of this apparition who only half an hour earlier had been a genial roughneck of a man named John McFarland.

"Bradley—"

"We're on our way—" Sheldon began, and glanced over at Marie.

"You're not going anywhere!" He jutted out the pistol straight for Sheldon's face. Abruptly then he heeled around:

"Goddamit, Marie, I told you, get lost! You and Simona — both of you — get the hell out of here. Goddamit, out!"

10

Despite the shock, the bizarreness of this moment, being gun-confronted by a rampaging McFarland, Sheldon was almost thankful for the intrusion: for he and Simona had been on the taut edge of a bad row, another one, one that might have become as abrasive as the battle of this afternoon—the worst they'd ever had, and the loudest:

Simona, his first real fulfillment of love, was capable of outbursts that could stun him, those occasional gin-outbursts of hers when her Texas showed at the seams, could undo him for a full day or night or longer.

Or was he only seeking some flaw in her to justify his own weaknesses?

Or was he showing his age?

He who never felt or acknowledged the traces of

time? He who always held on to illusion, even though lately he had had to shut his eyes, his mind, to certain bruises, portents of the years:

Only once or twice. Yesterday, as he walked up the slope to Simona's house, there'd been that flash of faintness or dizziness and he'd had to grope for support against the trunk of the eucalyptus tree. It was all so quick he wasn't even sure it had happened. But he'd sought an immediate rationale: too many cigarettes, too much coffee before he'd left the hotel. This could happen even to athletes who indulged in excesses. . . .

But what had happened this afternoon between him and Simona could be more damaging than all the cigarettes and all the coffee in the world. . . .

Still, how glorious the day had begun, that drive up to the ancient walled village of St. Paul de Vence and going to the Foundation Maeght, the modern gallery that Simona called her favorite "art environment" with its profusion of Miro's works, and the great virile Calders on the emerald lawn and the pools with their mosaics by Braque. This morning they'd gone to see the exhibit of Bonnards, and (again) Simona had reveled not only in the court of Giacometti's gaunt and towering figures but in the Giacometti-designed door handles, display cases and even the ashtrays.

And they'd had a splendid lunch on the terrace of La Colombe d'Or and later when they got back they'd fallen gloriously into bed sharing, as they always did, the daily crossword puzzle, and then sharing something much better: each other. Except that today. . . .

No, that had nothing to do with age. That sort of thing happened to him now and then, didn't it? Men were vulnerable, and Simona knew this, and after the foolish disaster in bed she had reassured him, she ¹ ad urged him to forget it. But despite her understanding he'd allowed his fears to surface. And later at the end of the martini-time, that awful battle had started simply because he'd said, "Keep your voice down, Simona, you don't have to *shout.*"

"You mean you don't want to hear!" She'd turned impatiently, her long amber hair still not put up, hanging loose, tangled from the hour in bed. He, however, had already showered and dressed. It was after five. They were due at the McFarlands at 7:30. And he'd wanted to dedicate himself to his last drink, to his private way of phasing out all that had been disagreeable a moment ago. "You don't want to hear. And I guess I haven't really wanted to either. All I ever did was believe what I wanted to believe about you, and goddamit, Sheldon, you're wonderful and I love you, but now I wonder if you're not too wonderful, maybe you're just not true! I keep asking myself how can any man be like this. And now I know, I think I know."

"What do you know?"

She poured herself more gin; her words were slurring and she didn't seem to be listening to him, only staring at him, talking, shouting at him. "Your trouble, you want to know what your trouble is? It's that you're afraid to live, I mean live life the way it is — live with *reality*. All this time I've only seen one side of you — the side you wanted me to see. And suddenly I realize I only know half a man. I don't really know you. I still don't. I know nothing about you. You have a son and you won't talk about him. You had a wife, and never a word. A mother, who the hell was she? Nothing. And all the time I keep asking myself who is he, what is he?" Simona, still barefoot, was moving across the old planked flooring of the living room, she finished her gin and added a few more drops to her glass, holding the bottle very carefully. She turned back to him, and he could see how sharply she drew in her breath and then released the words. "I don't know who you are. But something about you isn't real. Even your holing up in the Hotel de Paris all summer long — with your own personal towels and sheets so nobody else's dirt gets mixed up with yours — oh, shit, Sheldon. You skim across life — life's been good to you — but I wonder if you've ever really tasted, touched it, if you've ever suffered—really—"

"And you're in the process of making sure I do, is that it?"

"Oh, shit! Don't give me that! Sometimes you drive me up a wall with your 'not so loud, Simona, lower your voice, Simona'! You're flesh and blood like the rest of us. You're a man, Sheldon, you're not

Peter Pan. It's as if you were scared shitless to let
yourself go. And you can't even stand it when *I* let
myself go. But when I scream or shout, Sheldon, it's
because there's something inside of me that has to
come out! It means I'm alive. I'm trying in my own
dumb way to reach out — but you — I don't think I
ever really reach you, Sheldon. Sometimes I don't
even know how, or why, I love you—"

"Louder, can't you make it louder — " Sheldon
scarcely recognized his own voice. "I really appreciate everything you're telling me — you don't
know why you love me! But all I talked about at
lunch today was us, our getting married—"

"Marriage — who needs it! Maybe all you were
talking about at lunch was Sheldon Bradley. But I
don't even know who Sheldon Bradley is!"

"Damn it. Can't you lower your voice? Can't you
speak in a — can't we just talk, do we have to get to
this—"

"Oh, screw you, baby! You want soft voices, go
back to all those make-believe little drawing rooms
with all those make-believe phony little cunts! But
count me out!"

The way his chest was pounding, his hoarseness,
the sweat hot on his forehead, suddenly caused
Sheldon to turn away from her and move shakily out
of the house; he sank down in a garden chair, he held
his head between his hands: he was crazy with despair, with resentment of this shrill battle, her abrasive gin-boosted words. That was one thing about

Marie, her voice; it had that softness, the grace notes of innocence beneath, and that could somehow always soothe him. Why was he so sensitive to sound? Why, to this day, would he still shudder remembering the shrillness of Lennie Levine's father? Why had he been so attentive when Mr. Trowbridge or Mr. Andrews spoke in those modulated tones? Yes, even though the woman he'd married, Elizabeth, with her prayer-like voice, turned out to be a malicious harridan, and he'd ended up praying she would never open her mouth again . . . .

Simona's outburst—did it betray her true feelings? And if they were her true feelings he knew he would lose her, and he didn't know how to tell her, how to explain to her or anyone else in the world that he was not what she insisted he was. Or that if he was why shouldn't he live with it: if illusion was so imperative to him, why couldn't he choose to live with it: who the hell could live without illusion, or even delusion? Each of us had our spectres, terrors, why couldn't we cope with them as best we could in our own ways. . . .

Shit:

She'd kept saying it over and over. How could she transform herself into a demon like this? Was it the liquor that made her attack him? Could liquor in some way make her more psychic or intuitive about his deceptions. . . . ?

And the terrible pain in his chest now, in his throat, in his eyeballs, pain unbearable because he knew that Simona had pushed him face to face with the one person he didn't want to see: himself.

He'd wanted desperately to tell her about himself, he'd wanted to tell her and rid himself of the weight on his heart. He couldn't or wouldn't because all he could remember was how Elizabeth used the truth after they'd married, how it often had spiked arguments and rancor between them, and how she had used it as a weapon against him.

And even though Simona was in no way like Elizabeth, he still feared telling her anything that might flaw or threaten the one near-perfect relationship he'd finally found.

If only the pounding would go away.

And why did Simona have to keep after him, stir him up like this: didn't she know by now that he had always flourished not on the coarse-grained wood of life, but on its patina. . . .

When he had finally regained a measure of calm, he rose and walked back into the house. He found Simona in the bedroom putting up her hair. And drinking black coffee.

"I'm not going to go to the McFarlands'. I'll call Marie and tell her not to expect me. You—"

Simona turned away from the dressing table mirror. "Sheldon."

She reached out and put her arms around his legs and rested her head against his groin, and then she looked up at him. "Sheldon — it's — I love you — I wish I could—"

He didn't need to hear any more, this was enough, this unexpected balm of the voice, the same voice he'd condemned, that had sent him fleeing, that had churned his insides, sent the fire through his bloodstream. . . .

As he felt her holding him, he did something he had never done during the entire span of his manhood: he began to cry. And he was so ashamed that he drew away from her and went, as if to hide, back into the living room and bent his head, leaning it against the cold stone fireplace.

Simona followed him and stood beside him, close to him. She didn't speak. She kissed him, a kiss of contrition now. From the tender way she pressed his hand it seemed she was telling him how she regretted her boozed-up outburst. Yet when she did speak: "Sheldon—I'm glad it happened. I mean, I'm glad I got it all out, and I hope you understand. I didn't want to hurt you, I was trying to help you, help *us*. Do you understand what I mean?"

He said yes he understood. But since the truth of it was so painful he preferred to hear no more. At least not now. . . .

He knew that sometime, somewhere, somehow, he would have to answer all the unanswered questions. But he had to put time between now and the day she

would confront him again. God help him then. But
now. . . .

They drove into Monte Carlo and arrived half an
hour late at the Residence du Parc.

He parked the car in the subterranean garage of the
building. And after locking the doors, he turned to
her and, with misguided aggressiveness, asked her
again to marry him.

It was too late or too soon; somehow he saw from
her still troubled face that he should not have
spoken.

"Not now, Sheldon. It's not important."

"Not important?" He stared at her in mute incom-
prehension. They were moving toward the elevator
and it seemed they were suddenly like two strangers.
It was as if they were walking with an unseen or
alien person between them.

"Excuse me—Sheldon—sorry. I—" John McFarland,
as if for the first time, was conscious of the pistol in
his hand: the sight was like an instant sedative; he
stood rooted on the marble terrace. "Jesus, what the
hell is happening to me—" He thrust the weapon
into his pants pocket. He looked at Sheldon and
shook his head. "Have to excuse me, Sheldon."
Another interval, a cigarette; "Have to tell you what's
going on—"

Sheldon was only now grasping the metamorphosis of this volatile man who, in the course of one evening, had been a clown and a maniac.

"Christ — " McFarland glanced back toward the living room. "Christ, where is everybody?" Then: "Let's get over to the other side. Have to talk to you."

The force of the man's anxiety was powerful, though Sheldon couldn't fathom why it should focus on him. The two men moved around the corner of the terrace.

"We've got to have a private talk, my friend." Though McFarland was in command of his poise, the siege of anger had left his face inflamed.

But when Sheldon heard the preliminary account of the loss of the Canadian subsidiary and the back taxes now due the United States Government, he could readily sympathize with the harassed arms dealer.

"—and when I got hold of Kevin he let me down. His capital is tied up for six months and my deal starts next Monday afternoon in Prague." McFarland jabbed his thumbs into his belt.

And Sheldon was again struck by the golden buckle which somehow looked incongruous on McFarland, this need to flaunt the Gucci *G* was probably his way of saying he was a part of the life his wife admired. Like certain Jews who . . .

"Now hear me, Sheldon, my friend. I'm going to level with you. This is between us. We are men who know how to keep things to ourselves." And then with a faint echo of the midway barker: "Tell me, do you know where you can get sixteen percent on your money? I said sixteen percent!"

"No, of course not." Sheldon was still mystified. "Why?"

"I'll tell you why. Because the IRS took you to the cleaners. You took a miserable beating on your capital gains tax in the States. Right?"

"A considerable amount, yes. But—"

"That's why I think you wouldn't object to packing in sixteen percent on a loan. Right?"

Sheldon finally grasped it: "A loan—?"

"Five hundred thousand. Say for ninety days. But I have to have it no later than Friday."

"John, surely you must understand that I—"

"You've got it sitting right here in M.C., Sheldon."

Sheldon loathed these kinds of confrontations, having to discuss money with friends. "John, I wish I could help you—sixteen percent is very generous— but right now I'm not in the position to make a gambling investment."

"Am I reading you right? You mean you're worried about me. You don't trust me?"

"John, half a million dollars is a lot of money in anybody's bank." But McFarland kept his harsh, questioning eyes on him.

"In other words," McFarland said it for him, "you're worried about my collateral?"

"Well, that goes without saying. But you see—"

"See what?"

"John, you're, to say the least, in a pretty damn irregular business. I doubt any bank would—"

"Let me help you out, Sheldon. What you're worried about is my life. But I'm not. What you're telling me is that it's strictly a question of collateral. Right?" McFarland stepped closer to him. "Listen, Sheldon, I've got to have that cash. You're a man who knows the difference between chicken shit and chicken salad. So we can be honest with each other. Okay?"

Sheldon nodded.

"Okay. Then I can tell you I'm offering you sixteen percent interest even though your kid, that son of yours out in L.A., worked for my brother and screwed him, or tried to screw him out of enough money to— okay, he wants to get into the movie business, and Kevin has the connections, his company is in there. But your kid doesn't get anywhere except in trouble. He's a sick kid. When I heard about it from my brother I told him to forget it, and Kevin quashed the case."

"My—" Sheldon faltered, words shriveled and lay parched on his tongue.

He seemed to hear only fragments of what McFarland was telling him. " — that kid of yours tried to defraud Kevin out of certain in-coming checks. Your smart son used the company stamp and deposited the checks in his own bank account. Kev put the dicks on him, he was booked straight for the slammer. That's where I came in. Because of you. And your kid's been on probation ever since last January."

Sheldon braced himself against the railing of the

terrace: "I—I can't believe that," he stammered, but
he could believe it, he'd always known or feared that
the boy's hostility — boy! God, he was twenty-five
now. He'd always feared something like this would
happen, the psychiatrist had warned him of it, the
danger of his son's hostilities. "I can't believe it,"
Sheldon heard himself say again. "I heard he was
working for a film distributor, but I didn't have any
idea it was your—"

"Listen, Sheldon, I would never have mentioned it
but when I saw how worried you were about the
goddam collateral—"

"You've known this—"

"Forget it. I never even told Marie. Why should I?
To her, to us, you're top stuff, a good friend. We all
live in the same town and Monte Carlo is smaller
than a small town. You learn to keep your mouth shut
around here. I know what you're up against with this
boy. Why should I add misery to misery?"

"All this time—" Sheldon kept watching him, looking for some sign of assurance he could hold on to.
"All this time you've known and you've never mentioned it? Not ever? Not to anyone?"

"To no one."

Sheldon said, "Very few people are that decent—"

"It isn't a question of decency. It's not that I'm a
nice guy with a great big mashed-potato heart. It's
something else."

"Oh?" Sheldon gripped the railing.

At first what McFarland was relating seemed ir-
relevant, another boring war story; but it wasn't. In

Korea, McFarland had become privy to what his superior, a Major Colbee, was getting away with at the base seventeen miles outside Seoul: he was selling U.S. gasoline, and he was stealing and selling weapons from our own arsenal. McFarland had caught him at it bare-handed — Colbee and a tech sergeant and a few poor black buck privates who today were no longer quite as poor.

"I learned the value of leverage. By accident. I didn't squeal on Colbee because you might say my staying alive was up to him. But when I saw how much gravy was being passed around I decided some of it might as well go to McFarland. And when the war was dragging to an end I wanted to get the hell out and be the first civilian to grab up the surplus. So I had a little talk with Colbee. Believe me, I got one of the fastest honorable discharges in the history of the Pacific theatre. And later I got my hands on enough weapons to sell at ten times what I paid. That's how your friend McFarland got into this business. But as I said, Sheldon, I've kept my crazy Irish mouth shut; I've learned it's smart to be dumb. I would have stayed dumb forever. But now suddenly I have to discuss this with you and tell you what I would have preferred to keep to myself. And that, Sheldon, is going to have to be your collateral."

For twenty-four hours Sheldon could not get himself to leave his rooms in the Hotel de Paris. He tortured himself with every possible option or alternative he could think of though he must have known that in the end he would have to yield.

Forgetting other people, forgetting even Simona, what this was all about was himself: his persona.

All these years he had kept his son outside the frame of his life; for all intents and purposes, he had no son:

Now, suddenly, this son was not only part of him again but had reappeared as a criminal, and it had to be John McFarland who knew it. . . .

The sordid slur on Sheldon's existence was unbearable; it might not wreck other men or other fathers, but it would surely destroy him. And he found no solace in saying that in an age already anesthetized by crime and immorality, who would give a damn what his son had done.

None of this could give him comfort. He knew he could never disassociate himself from this loathesome product of his own blood; just as he could not share this knowledge with the rest of the world—just as he would never be able to rid himself of the ever-growing burden of his own guilt. . . .

As for the money—it didn't matter. Nor could he really reproach McFarland. In fact, the arms trader had in Sheldon's eyes in some way grown in stature. After all, the bitter truth was that the nightmare was not of McFarland's making. It was his own.

And deep in his being he had spawned a new fear: that the nightmare was not over, that this was not the end of it. His stomach told him this, the way it felt now, and his chest—that same pain, slight, very slight, but always present. Indigestion. Acute indigestion.

Sheldon moved back to the high windows again and stared unseeingly down to the sea and the palm trees and the rococo Casino. . . .

No, all this was was fear; he had psyched himself into it. He had a way, didn't he, of psyching himself out or into the most extreme conditions. . . .

He'd been alone too long. He had to clear out of the hotel. Simona had called him twice. She was frantic with remorse: she was sure he'd stayed away because of the indignities she'd put him through.

And he'd let her think it. He simply could not bring himself to tell her the truth.

And he could not bring himself to stay away from her. He needed her. God, how he needed to see her, feel her, be with her, hear her: Simona was life; she was life itself and if he was letting death get near him Simona surely would banish it.

PART III *August*

Monte Carlo during the high season of August 1975 seemed in many ways a defiance of the world itself. Or so I felt after an absence of only two weeks. I had been to London for meetings with my English publisher and while there I had seen at first hand the austerity and the grim economic woes afflicting Great Britain.

Thus, upon my return to Monte Carlo with a somewhat more jaundiced view of man's future, I was forcibly struck by the lavish way money was being spent: the profits of the Casino were at an all time high; Princess Grace's Red Cross gala had enjoyed a record attendance (at 125 dollars per plate); beaches and discotheques abounded with "society" and film superstars; the hotels were booked to capacity.

155

Even though some of the more frivolous souls in Monte Carlo that summer were paying lip service to the monetary crisis toward which we might be heading, a new wave of big spenders was acquiring all the real estate their laundered money could buy. Even Nick began to show an unfamiliar flourish of mild prosperity: first class apartments and villas were renting for from five to fifteen thousand dollars per month. A turn for the best since his private caper with the Internal Revenue Service was surely doomed to a premature death.

Meanwhile, regardless of the rampant imbalance among the haves and the have-nots of the world, here in Monte Carlo the gustatory delights, solid or liquid, were an unending pageant of moveable feasts; parties went on around the clock; gambling was virtually non-stop; private yachts were docked hull-to-hull in the harbor.

It was now, during the zenith of summer, that Monaco's cornucopia of cultural goodies lavished forth: the starlit concerts in the palace courtyard, the symphonic orchestras led by distinguished guest conductors, the chamber groups, the plays, films and ballet; and, on a somewhat less exalted level, those evenings of al fresco dining and dancing and the cabaret productions featuring outstanding British, French and American performers. . . .

Despite, or perhaps because of, the doleful warnings of our political savants, our philosophical gurus, our funereal economists, this principality, ig-

nited by the high octane of the Riviera sun, kept fueling the entire range of one's appetites, from the esthetic to the carnal; these few princely acres kept erupting with a fierce and golden fire of hedonism.

I was reminded that similar extravaganzas and revelries in Monte Carlo had also marked the eras just prior to World War I and World War II.

Occasionally I had the uneasy vision that many of us were dancing at the edge of a chasm, refusing to look down, refusing to see what might be happening tomorrow.

And later I was to ask myself if it was the fear of tomorrow that caused Sheldon's sudden illness? Could it have been this same anxiety that made Nick turn in his U.S. passport with such haste — as if to beat the clock, to avoid any second thoughts on becoming an ex-American?

II

As an ex-American Nick felt a genuine sense of personal victory, and though the new feeling may not have been the high he'd anticipated, he would not quibble.

That long down-trip he'd been on with the U.S.A. was over.

He had made his statement. And if nobody quite went along with him, with the possible exception of Simona, that was all right with him. It had to be.

"Nick"—a voice, Janet Babcock's, reached him as he was starting out of the noontime bar of the hotel. "Are you in a big rush?"

"Small rush."

"Oh, that's right. The regatta."

He nodded: via Frederico, Alma had invited him to join them on the yacht of friends who had driven up into the hill country for the day. Frederico announced there would be lunch on the boat and then they would be following the annual Cannes-Monte Carlo Regatta.

"Well," Janet was saying, "I won't hold you up, Nick. I just wanted to tell you that she finally made it. I mean my sister. She got in early this morning."

"That's pretty underwhelming, Janet." Nick was relieved. He was very fond of Janet. But since her sister's trip had been delayed, she had stayed on in M.C. all those weeks, making that human error of not leaving the party until it was over. Now with her sister here, Nick knew he'd be seeing much less of Janet. The good dentist, Babcock, had accepted all this because he knew that Janet hadn't seen her sister in over three years and that this European vacation was something they'd been planning for a long time.

"Anyway, Nick," Janet was saying, "she's here. Absolutely shot . . . jet lag and all that extra work she's been doing in the States."

Marion Stokes, he saw, was coming in from the street and he politely deferred his departure for another minute:

Yes. Jet lag. Overwork. It was there on her face, in her walk.

This is Harper Nicholson. Nick.

How do you do.

Lemon hair, short and straight.

"Is this place for real?" Marion asked him.

Eyes gray, flecks of lightest blue. Taller and thinner than Janet. Same candid smile. . . .

"Janet said you'd hate it here," Nick recalled.

"That wouldn't be difficult. But oddly enough," Marion said, "from what little I've seen this morning, it's just what I need. Pure escape." Then: "I know a lot about you."

"I know an item or two about you."

"Like what?"

Like she went through Ohio State in three years; got her M.A. at University of Southern California; was now working on her study of American Indians in New Mexico — a doctorate that would lead to an associate professorship at U.S.C. But he said: "Like you're the black sheep of the family, a dangerous guerrilla who's out to overthrow the United States government, turn it back to the Indians and marry the Big Chief."

"Nick, have you got time for a coke or some coffee?" Janet asked.

"No, wish I did. Have to take off."

"Have you any tips for us?" Marion asked. "I understand you know your way around the neighborhood."

He nodded. "Watch out what you say when you write home. The CIA is screening all picture postcards."

"You're a big help," Marion said.

"*Ciao.*" Nick was on his way.

"*Ciao* . . ." Janet's farewell echoed in the marble lobby.

Nick paused on the steps witnessing the August chaos: he was always fascinated by the way the doorman of this celebrated hotel maneuvered all the cars for which there was so little parking space, this doorman who proudly wore in the lapel of his uniform the decoration bestowed upon him by Prince Rainier, this man born in Monaco, who manipulated Rolls-Royces and Bentleys and Chevrolets and Cadillacs as if they were toys, who knew which owner deserved which space and for how long — it was a kind of automotive ballet, and he'd been at it for over twenty-five years; he had often been kind to Nick, passing on hints about new arrivals who might be likely candidates for real estate ventures. Nick waved to the doorman who waved back and who went to the stone balustrade of the steps, pressed a button which would light up the signal in the Casino park taxi stand, and within seconds a taxi swung around to pick up the fare and the doorman received his gratuity. The cabbies in Monte Carlo had to pay a goodly sum to the principality to acquire this lucrative location.

It wasn't until half an hour later, when Nick was on the boat having drinks with Alma A and Frederico, that he stopped in mid-swallow and damn near choked with the sudden and belated realization that Janet's sister Marion reminded him of someone else:

of Jane; and the resemblance was uncanny! Oh, why in hell did he have to rush out of the hotel and how could he have been so wiseass and unhelpful and rude with that poor, knocked-out, far-from-home, slim-waisted, long-legged brainie who'd just been sprung from some New Mexico Indian reservation and who ought to be given the courtesy of, at the very least, one of those old Harper Nicholson tours, complete with spiel.

And yes she was carrying a camera, too, a real hard-core tourist. But the only Indians she would see around here wore saris or had a diamond in their nostril. . . .

Why in hell did he have to rush off?

For this? This eighty-eight foot, two-masted schooner? For this elegant lunch being served on the aft deck as the boat sailed out to sea. . . .

For this?

No. For the talk with Frederico who had come up with a piece of intelligence which he was eager to discuss with Nick.

After a crew member removed the high crystal vase of flame-colored gladiolas from the table, a steward served the champagne and the lobster salad.

Alma A put the lunch away with gusto: unlike most people partial to booze, she was also an unabashed gourmet; when she wasn't drinking she was in the kitchen cooking joyfully. Frederico had complained that he had put on more than six pounds this summer. After lunch, the vodka and wine claimed Alma and she took her statuesque self below deck for a nap. But today, Nick had observed, she was not coming on with her customary sunny face; today she was eating more and definitely drinking more. Why?

"Why? That's what we have to talk about, Nick, why I wanted to get you on the boat. So we can talk." Frederico leaned forward in the canvas chair. Shirtless, a gold chain with the gold medal of the Virgin shone sacredly against his splendid bronzed and brawned chest. "Alma—this morning when I called you, she was already like half stoned. A letter from her husband. Herb is not getting back to M.C. He's already put it off twice. Now he's not coming at all. And suddenly Alma doesn't like it. I ask her why. She is a clam. Not a word. But I know what it is. It's this chick Herb has. He used to see her only once in a while but now it's like every night. I know it. Alma knows it. She's in bad shape and I thought I'll get Nick and we'll try to talk her into going back to the States and selling the place here. If we can talk her into it."

"You're her boy, Frederico. Why do you need me?"

"Because you can say it nicer."

Nick contemplated the distant jagged shoreline of Monaco. The regatta was scheduled for two o'clock.

"What we have to do, Nick, is get her on that plane. The only thing is how do we work it about the apartment?"

The problem was a new one for Nick. He groped for some kind of solution, but it eluded him. It occurred to him finally that he might draw up a private agreement, legal in these parts, in which Alma promised to give Sheldon Bradley first option to buy in the event she put the apartment up for sale. . . .

"Yeah. That might work. If you—"

"Not me, Frederico. You. You're the one who has to get her signature. No, let's forget it. It's not the way I like to do business."

"Listen, don't cop out on me now, Nick. You just write it up and I'll try to do the rest."

Reluctantly Nick yielded. And on a sheet of the yacht's stationery he composed the agreement, a literary effort which might well go down as a minor masterpiece in the annals of Monaco real estate.

By the time Alma A was back on deck she had to have two vodkas to wake her up enough to have black coffee, except that she never got around to the coffee.

And Nick, inspired by the sudden prospect of his commission in the event of the sale to Sheldon, brought the talk around to Herb Ainsworth. "I was asking Frederico what's been bothering you, Alma—I know you're not yourself today — and Frederico seems to think you're worried about Herb—"

Alma A added another slug to her empty glass. "You're damn well right it's Herb. That stinker!"

"Now wait a minute, Alma," Nick said, "before you go calling him a stinker, you ought to find out for yourself if anything's wrong. Maybe it's all in your imagination, and if nothing is wrong—"

"No ifs or buts. I know."

"She knows." Frederico hammered it home, subtlety not being one of his notable assets.

"Let me tell you something, Nick," she said. "I've never worried about Herb or what he does. He knows how I feel. I've always told him: 'Herb, I don't care how or where you get your appetite, as long as you come home to eat.' "

"That's a fact," contributed Frederico.

"Frederico, my darling, did anyone ask your opinion? Please shut up."

"Listen, Alma, don't talk to me like—"

"Alma, this is none of my business" — Nick was pursuing it now—"but I think we've been friends long enough that I can say that if I were you I'd stay right here in M.C. and forget Herb. If he wants to get himself involved with some young broad, let him. He'll get it out of his system, four or five years from now he'll start forgetting she's even alive."

"*Four or five years?* Are you insane, Nick?" She took an indignant sip of vodka and followed it with a proper gulp.

"Maybe six or seven years," Nick said. "What's the difference, Alma? You know when it's finally over, he'll come crawling back to you."

"That's what happened with this uncle of mine in Bridgeport," Frederico related a bit too exuberantly. "He took off with some young chick and my aunt went like crazy. But you know something, one day she just tracked him down and took a stand. You know what happened? The next day he shows up and begs my aunt to take him back. So now after only about ten years he's back in the saddle."

"Frederico I am not interested in your uncle in Bridgeport. I'm only interested in my husband in New York."

Nick reached for the nearest cliché: "Give him enough rope and he'll hang himself, Alma."

"Oh, that stinker!"

"Now don't get yourself too exercised about this. He'll come to his senses one of these days—" Nick paused, he had a slight fever of remorse, handing out this bullshit; yet he knew enough about Herb and the marriage and what it meant to both of them, to feel that Alma's returning to the States was about the only constructive option she had: marriages fall apart easily but it takes a calculated effort and action to put them together again. "Believe me, Alma, he'll get the message."

"But when, Nick?" She was into the vodka and no mistake. "When? I'll tell you when. When I'm a ghastly vegetable in some grisly nursing home in some godforsaken swamp in New Jersey—"

"Alma," advised Nick, the sage marriage counselor, "men have periods like menopause and they sometimes get scared they're losing their machismo. If you just stay here and hang loose he'll get to feeling so guilty you won't be able to keep him away."

"Hey—I don't know about that!" Frederico gave him a look of darkest warning. "Listen, Nick, how do you know he'll feel guilty? He and Alma have a great marriage. What are you trying to do, blow it?"

"He's trying to help me, can't you see that, Frederico?" Alma protested. "Or do you want me to make a drawing for you?" Then: "You were saying, Nick? You're bright, you've got a head on you. You don't get your life fuzzed up the way I do. I drink too much. I'm going on the wagon next week."

A familiar refrain.

"Actually," Nick tacked around to another direction, "actually, Alma, it isn't as if you have a problem like some women I know. After all, it isn't as if Herb is a pauper."

"You can say that again. That's what drives me insane. How do I know where his money is going? How do I know this little tart isn't taking—"

"Nonsense." Nick at last saw the light, and the light glowed like money. "In the first place, I imagine that like most people we know, you and Herb own everything jointly—"

"Some things, yes. But the Sutton Place house is still in his name from his first marriage, and the apartment here is in mine. But I'm not about to stand by and let some little bitch get her hands on that house in New York. I spent two years of my life decorating it, and what it's worth today, after all I've done to it—"

"Yes." Slowly and obliquely Nick led her around to the matter of how to dispose of her apartment in the event she decided to return to the States. "And if you ever do decide to sell, you won't have to pay a capital gains tax here and you can get the money any way you want it, Uncle Sam will never know the difference, and think of all the guns he would have manufactured with your tax money."

"Nick, I'm stoned, I know it. But I don't buy that nonsense about guns. If I sell I sell, and if I do, which I doubt, I doubt if I sell . . . " Her words were beginning to run together. "I trust you to put the money in the right place so I can put my little hands on it."

"Frankly, Alma, I can't see you unloading that pad. In five years from now it'll be worth—"

"In five years from now how do I know where I'll be? As you yourself said before"—she had another touch of vodka—"Nick, I'm glad we're having this talk. But I'm not going to take your advice. I'm not going to just sit here on my big derrière and let that stinker get away with this, not with—not with . . . " It was Alma's last utterance of the day.

By the time the yacht was back in the harbor of Monte Carlo it was five o'clock. And Nick realized he had scarcely even seen the regatta. . . .

But mainly what he wanted to see was Janet's sister.

As soon as possible.

Sooner.

But he didn't even know her.

If he didn't even know her why did he have to see her?

Back at his station at the bar he used the phone. No answer in Janet's room.

Less than an hour later Frederico was calling him. "Nick—she signed it! I got her to sign it! And you know something"—he was tripping over the sticky words of his greed—"she knew what she was doing and she said she knew what you were doing too. Stoned and all. But she said you helped her make up her mind. You can start the deal. She wants the bread. And me too, don't forget. I want my slice."

Nick recovered enough to ask if there was any mention of price.

Six hundred and fifty thousand dollars. All in Swiss currency. "We're all set and you can go sing along with Sheldon."

Immediately Nick called Bradley's suite. He was out. He tried Simona's house. Out.

He called Janet again. In.

"How's everything, Janet?"

"This morning was the first time I've seen you in three days, Nick. You might have telephoned yesterday or—"

"I'm calling now, Janet, to see if you're free for dinner."

"In other words, you mean is Marion free?"

"Why would you say a thing like that?" Nick tried to put conviction behind his voice but it came out about as honest as a slot machine.

"Why? I don't know. Just a hunch. I hate my hunches, Nick. They're usually right."

"Janet, for godsakes, I only saw her for half a minute."

"I know."

"Well?"

"Well, okay. I'm jealous. I hate jealousy like I hate hunches."

"Can't we meet for dinner?"

"How was the regatta?"

"What regatta?"

"Dinner is perfectly okay." Then: "I assume you mean both of us."

"Yes."

"Well . . . "

"Well what?"

"What am I supposed to say?" Janet asked.

"I don't know."

"Well . . . " There was a more prolonged hesitation. "I suppose — even if it kills me — I ought to say it couldn't happen to a nicer guy. All right?"

12

"You couldn't have given us nicer weather, Sheldon. New York was unbearable for the past week." Judge and Mrs. Benjamin Skillman stopped by his table at the Summer Sporting Club: They were old friends of his. They came to Monte Carlo every year for two weeks at the Old Beach Hotel. Judge Skillman sat on the bench of the New York Superior Court; as for Rusty Skillman, it was said that the only address book she used was the *New York Social Register*. They'd called Sheldon earlier and tomorrow night they would all be going to the symphonic concert being given in the courtyard of the palace.

As soon as they left Sheldon said, "Your face, Simona, was such a dead giveaway."

"Well, look, Sheldon, they're perfectly nice people. It's just that I've had that bit. I know they adore you, I know you helped him raise funds for the Philharmonic. But really, Sheldon, isn't life too short?"

"Much too short." He watched the Skillmans as they went around the great circle of the room, as they passed the table of John and Marie McFarland. "I will say," Sheldon admitted, "they seem more starchy these days."

"And you, baby, seem a lot less starchy." Simona covered his hand with hers.

"Are you trying to bring out the worst in me, Simona?"

"Trying like hell. I adore you."

During dinner they discussed the apartment. He would take possession October fifteenth. And he had already yielded to her suggestion that he mix antiques with contemporary furniture and art. He'd always been too orthodox or inflexible in his taste. Yes, another step forward.

But then if he examined his life he realized it had always taken some special event, or person to galvanize him into a new phase or into a new milieu. It had always been like that with him:

Out of college his encyclopedic knowledge of philately had led to a job with a stamp and coin company in New York. And during those three years with that company he had embellished, enriched his own collection and he had found a buyer for it: a wealthy and

eccentric antiques dealer from Woodbury, Connecticut. This gentleman not only offered Sheldon more
money, but the opportunity to learn a new trade. This
had been Sheldon's introduction to Americana. And
when the dealer died two years later, Sheldon took
himself out of the countryside and straight to B.
Altman's department store at 34th Street and Fifth
Avenue in New York City. He got the job he was
seeking, and just fourteen months later, he was made
assistant buyer of Early American furniture and not
long after that he became the head of the entire
department. In those days B. Altman's was known for
their excellent selection of early American antiques.
And with these antiques he lived, and he soon began
to identify with them, along with American folk art—
the portraits, banners, trade signs, weathervanes. Between 1944 and 1950 he lived with his empathy for
these pieces, these vestiges of America's New England heritage: the furniture and artifacts of this world
had become his family.

He left B. Altman's because he was ready to enter a
new phase: the restoration of eighteenth-century
American buildings. And he filled an entire
warehouse with random width floorboards, maple-
and pine-panelled doors, wall panelling, hand-
wrought nails and hardware. All his savings went into
that warehouse. He could have drawn from memory
the landmark houses and churches in Salem or Dux-
bury or Boston or Litchfield or Deerfield. . . .

It would never have occurred to Sheldon that he might ever abandon his passion for Early Americana. But that's what happened after he met Elizabeth Claridge, the woman he married. He'd gone out to Old Westbury, Long Island, to her family's estate to bid on the lumber of the barn and stables which were going to be torn down:

He'd lost the bid, won Elizabeth. Or, as it turned out, she won him; or more accurately, they both lost. At any rate she was the one who proposed marriage, not he. Elizabeth did not possess the kind of chemistry or beauty that could excite or overwhelm him. She did possess a landmark heritage:

Her great-grandfather founded the Wall Street investment banking firm which was continued by her grandfather and by her father; two of her brothers were still on the firm's board of directors. The Long Island estate and the Fifth Avenue duplex of Elizabeth's family were treasure troves of 17th- and 18th-century English and French furniture, and Sheldon found himself suddenly challenged and fascinated by these collections, most of which were heirloom pieces. His instinct for fine antiques expanded and he began to see a whole new esthetic horizon; and a personal involvement in a first-rate tradition: Elizabeth had ingrained appreciation for these heirlooms and she had a considerable knowledge of them but it wasn't long before he acquired the same expertise and sure judgment about European antiques that he'd had about works of Americana.

Elizabeth's origins were impeccable; and granted that she might not have had a sculpted or classic sort of profile, or that her chestnut hair was too thin and dry, she carried herself with admirable authority and she spoke with authority in a dulcet voice which Sheldon took comfort in, never dreaming that this softness, this genteel voice of hers would be used in a poisonous way to undermine him.

There was something else about her he did not know in the beginning. They'd been at the opera one night and afterward, without warning, she'd suggested that she would like to marry him. It was in the taxi and he was thankful that it was dark enough to conceal both his surprise and the ambivalence of his feelings. What he had no way of knowing then was that Elizabeth was in love with another man, a doctor, who had rejected her, and in her despair, on the rebound, she was determined to capture another man: Sheldon.

Because he couldn't bring himself to answer her spontaneously and because, frankly, at that moment he was more impressed by who she was than by what she was, he decided to do something he'd never done before and would never do again: he told her he was Jewish. It was his way of trying to resolve his conflicting feelings about her — he suspected, or hoped, that it would persuade her to withdraw her interest in him.

It didn't. Elizabeth had been so emotional, so determined to prove something to herself, to the doctor who had fallen in love with another of his patients, to her own family and friends, that she probably would have married Sheldon even if he'd come by mail.

After she became pregnant she confessed to him that it had been the doctor she'd loved and still did. Sheldon's ego, his feelings, were battered. Still, he couldn't bring himself to leave her: she was, after all, carrying his child.

Her father (who reminded him almost poignantly of Andy Ward's father) came to his financial assistance, permitting him to buy into the business of Howard Mitchell, which was small, distinguished but unenterprising. By 1955, he and Mitchell had acquired the brick Georgian townhouse on Madison Avenue which became the site of their meteoric success.

One time, secure and established, Sheldon asked Elizabeth if she would have married him if it meant using his real name. "If you would have been Mrs. Samuel Bernstein?"

She had pondered the question: "Frankly, Sheldon, I doubt it."

He was not astonished. He could accept this.

Nonetheless, he suffered nights of insomnia, fearful that somebody besides her might discover what nobody else knew.

Despite all the compromises of his marriage, it

might have endured had not Sheldon Junior been born, or rather had not the boy, as he grew older, begun to develop characteristics that Sheldon, in the trauma of his youth, had found so unbearable. The boy in no way resembled Sheldon.

By the time his son was eight the marriage had completely deteriorated. It was during this time that the incident occurred to Sheldon Junior that ultimately destroyed what was left of the marriage.

The boy was at a new private school, and on his second day he met the athletic coach. Ironically the man's name happened to be Bradley. And he kept staring at Sheldon Junior and, in a variation of a similar confrontation in Sheldon's own boyhood, the man said: "I'm a Bradley too. And my family, we Bradleys, are spread all over the U.S.A., and I know most of them, we all keep up. I've never seen a Bradley like you though. But that's all right, son. Maybe we can use a little Jewish blood around here. Now get in there and stow your gear in your locker."

Sheldon was away when this happened. And when his son asked Elizabeth about it, she told him for the first time the whole Bradley myth. And she told it with venom.

After that the strained relationship that had developed between father and son totally cracked: the son inevitably felt he had been betrayed; Sheldon for his part felt that Elizabeth had betrayed him.

It became an unendurable household and ended in

divorce, with Elizabeth taking the boy.

After a while Sheldon tried to make another effort to show paternal affection or at least interest in the boy. He invited him to have lunch with him one Saturday. He also invited Elizabeth.

The boy, who arrived early at Sheldon's museum-like apartment, was wearing a dirty school baseball uniform, cap on his head and mitt on his hand. Elizabeth appeared just in time to hear Sheldon tell the boy to go to his old room, wash up before lunch.

When Sheldon Junior finally returned he was holding a giant pickle bent against his nose and in cruel assault began shouting at Sheldon: "You're a phony, you're a Jew! You're a phony, you're a Jew!"

Sheldon, who had never hit a living soul struck his own son in the face so that there was blood where the pickle had been. Elizabeth cried out, and Sheldon, in remorse, tried to take his son into the bathroom to wash away the blood but the boy wrenched himself free and ran out of the apartment, Elizabeth hurrying out after him.

That afternoon with his son was the blackest day since the blackest days of his own boyhood.

Sheldon was unmindful of the way the Summer Sporting Club had become excessively crowded. He and Simona were discussing the move into the Residence du Parc. Though he had not told her, he had had the apartment put in her name. A small testimony of his love, his belief in her: and he probably would never mention it until after they got married. If they got married. He simply couldn't imagine living in the Residence du Parc without her, without her as his wife: a very traditional view, yes; and though intellectually he might agree with her that marriage seemed somehow out of joint with the times, the old-fashioned fact was that he wanted to be married. And very much so. He drew from Simona an ineffable new kind of closeness with life. . . .

Two bottles between them, and a third on the way. Sheldon pushed back the rattan chair and rose. He left for the men's room. On his way back he paused to talk to Marie and John McFarland.

He'd seen the arms trader privately last week on his return from Eastern Europe and though there had been no mention of business, he could tell from his expansiveness, from the play of humor in the dark eyes, that the arms deal with the African Defence Minister was definitely shaping up to his satisfaction (and hence, hopefully, to Sheldon's). Also, there had been nothing on McFarland's rubicund face that in any way betrayed what had transpired between them on that traumatic night of Marie's dinner party. Secrets, Sheldon had decided, were a part of the man's existence, indispensable to his success: to know what other people didn't was what gave McFarland the "leverage" he so often referred to. Yet secrets were secrets, and now Sheldon knew he would have to live with fear and uncertainty.

"Have you seen Nick?" Marie asked. "He's over there at the bar. With his new friend."

"Well, I must say," Sheldon commented, "since he met Marion, I haven't seen much of him. He's certainly keeping her very much to himself. And I also must say, since I've seen Marion, I can't blame him."

"Those two are in the sack night and day and in between." McFarland enjoyed contemplating this image. Though Marie had not said a word, he turned to her: "Well, it's Nick's business, isn't it? If he wants to screw his head off I say God bless him." McFarland downed a bit of his whiskey. "Ah, Eros, and Nick in his prime!" The phrase rolled off his ready tongue with extravagant brogue and brio.

It wasn't until near midnight, as Sheldon and Simona left the dance floor, that Nick caught up with them:

"Sheldon, look, this love of my life insists on dancing with you."

"Flattery, Nick, is one of the lowest forms of human intercourse, and what's more, I welcome it any time."

Nick was grinning. "Marion thinks you're too good to be true."

"Are you?" Marion Stokes asked him as they went to the dance floor.

"Am I what?" The music, fortunately, was the kind he was at home with—Cole Porter.

"The other day when I finally met you, I mean when we had that long rap," Marion was saying, "I told Nick you couldn't be for real."

"Why not?" Marion Stokes felt young and fresh and Sheldon felt ancient and sluggish. He observed over her shoulder Simona watching him and there was a lovely bemused softness in her eyes. "Why do you think I'm not for real?"

"I don't know. You're so straight—I mean it the way it is: straight. In the best sense. Maybe I'm turned on by this because the way you are, a person who holds on to his values — there aren't many around these days, they're a vanishing breed."

"Like Indians?"

"Yes. Like Indians and"—but shortly the connection with her was broken: the band had finished their set and a new group came in and a new beat broke forth. Sheldon was the first to admit he was still not proficient in this most recent of imported dance crazes.

At any rate Marion would prefer going back to his table to continue their conversation.

The conversation turned out to be nonexistent.

The new group, a black combo, was playing the hustle and Nick and Simona were dancing to it. Of course they had rhythm built into their limbs, and soon their dancing became more like a performance;

gradually the floor emptied and the people were all standing around watching them.

"Do it! Do the hustle!" exhorted the bongo player.

Nick and Simona did it; they were a dazzling team, coupled up, in and out of each other's arms, fantastic footwork and energy. Their spins and dips grew more inventive and then they were tight together, arms thrust upward, hands clasped.

It was something Sheldon had never seen between the two, this sort of rhythmic chemistry, the response, the empathy of their bodies.

It was unbearable, this enviable display of intimacy, this easy, joyous knowledge of each other, this extension or evocation of their past lovemaking. . . .

Whatever it was, the dance went endlessly on, sickeningly endless. And Simona's eyes were a blaze of blueness. . . .

And the applause. Everyone applauded as if they had witnessed a spectacular *pas de deux* by Nureyev and Fonteyn. . . .

"What's the matter, Sheldon?" Simona broke the sullen quiet of the drive back into the hills.

"Not a thing." He was still fighting for control — angry as much with himself as with her. "Not a thing."

"Sheldon, what is it? And please, for godsakes, don't say it's because I danced with Nick."

"Did you have to make such a public spectacle of it?"

"Sheldon, you can't be serious—"

"I think you and Nick could do very well again. You ought to try going back on your old circuit together, peddling clothes and jewelry—"

"Oh, Sheldon, stop. All we did was dance. I haven't danced like that in years, it felt good for a change. That doesn't mean Nick and I—you make it sound like we were screwing in public. . . . "

"You might as well have been."

His own lovemaking, he knew, had not exactly been outstanding, not lately; Simona, he felt or imagined, was not altogether fulfilled; and though she had not even hinted at any possible discontent, their private life had, he felt, taken a subtle turn for the worst. . . .

"Oh, Sheldon, I just can't believe you're in such a sweat over absolutely nothing. Mygod, Nick and I—"

"You and Nick. That's what it was, that's what everyone was watching, and I had to watch it too . . ."

"Oh, shit, how can you talk like this, how can you think like this? God, Sheldon, will you never believe how much I love you? You still don't know what I'm like, you really don't know what I'm like at all—"

"I don't know *anything* anymore—" He said it in a voice that was almost impossible for him to identify as his own.

He slowed down the car. In her driveway, after he'd turned off the motor, they each sat as in far corners of a room:

Except there was no silence in the stillness of the

summer night, not the way his heart was beating. The throbbing rose up into his throat and ears and the persistent, pulsing pain he'd come to accept was not the same now:

A knife, a band of steel was strangling, garroting his chest and he gasped because there was no air, no air. . . .

"Simona—" but the word was lost, choked, suffocated; and he felt he was falling, his chest was crushed, crucified, and he plunged into the well of blackness.

13

There was nothing as lazily loving, drowsily erotic—
Nick addressed the sunless curvilinear nakedness of
Marion's back—nothing like it: they'd fallen asleep
this way and she'd dozed off, her hand between her
legs pressing him, not wanting him to withdraw:

After a brief space of sleep, she was stirring awake,
as was his most personal and best friend. And Marion
was stroking him all over, slowly, which was what
made it all so lazy and drowsy and loving. . . .

"Ohhh—" Her languorous murmur. "Oh, Nick . . ."

He pressed less sleepily against her, his hand curving around her lovely rump: while inside her he felt
himself swell and swell, growing hugely like the
dough of a slim limp croissant rising in the oven's
heat.

He felt her contract—no croissant was ever this
hard—and felt the tremor in her thighs:

"Nick, Nick—"

Yes? He stayed with it, baker and lover, and loving as he had never experienced it: and he had to sustain this all-time sensation—

He made one error, a beautiful one . . . he had drawn back just enough to watch himself, watch her, and the sight truly consumed him:

To see himself, to see this slow movement of their union, to see it and know it wasn't only an act of copulation but sex caught and exalted in the flush of love:

But god. The sight was too much. He had to look away, he had to concentrate on the back of her head, the lank pale yellow strands of her hair; but that's when there was that thrust, Marion's ass-end twitch, and that's when her murmuring grew into moans and into the cries of his name:

So that he had to reach her deeply, wedging himself fiercely against her and gloriously pumping all of him, his love, into her, this piston of his power and need unceasing until the clenching, almost catatonic burst of their coming.

They talked in darkness, she was in his arms and they talked about how it was, as if wanting to hold on and prolong and particularize all the sensations.

Marion turned on the lamp and reached for the cigarettes on the bedtable. And exactly as Jane had always done, she lit two cigarettes and gave him one and there were the twin glows that marked the smoker's post-coital interlude with a special satisfaction.

Marion Stokes and her sister Janet were the two different sides of the same parental coin. Janet had gone against the grain of the family's permissive, cultural way of life and had sought conventional security as a dentist's wife, only to find that the life was suffocating and the conventionality a facade for shoddy sex and other dubious diversions. And now Marion predicted her sister would be a candidate for a future existence on the Riviera.

As for Marion, she had not resisted her family's style. She admired her father, a lawyer, who gave much of his time to free legal counseling for underprivileged groups. Marion had become interested in some of these cases. When she was sixteen, one of her father's non-paying clients was a young Navaho Indian who was up on a charge of car theft, a crime he did not commit but which the prosecution easily won, playing on the Indian's color and his fierce, angry, monosyllabic way of talking on the witness stand. This young man's great-grandparents, Marion learned, had had their New Mexico pasturelands stolen from them by white men, and they had lost two of their small children during an enforced march in the spring of 1864. Marion's father was able to get this prison sentence reduced to five months, and when the Indian was released he worked for her family for over a year. He became one of her close friends. His horrendous tales about the lives of his parents and their parents and relatives aroused Marion's anger and pity and set the direction of her future. Like her father she could not be close to injustice without trying to rectify or mitigate it. But unlike her father she went beyond current cases and began to read whatever she could about the history of Indians and the more she read the more she wanted to investigate, probe.

One summer between her junior and senior year at Ohio State she and another student hitchhiked to California and ended up spending a week in Big Sur living in a kind of commune run by a Stanford University professor, an eccentric, whose erudition about Indian affairs included their music; and he would sit in front of his outdoor fire and with a hand-crafted flute of cherry wood would play unwritten or unrecorded Indian folk music. He taught these songs to Marion and the other acolytes in his circle. . . .

Nick, who considered himself fairly knowledgeable about minorities was, however, woefully ignorant about Indians and like many defenders of the downtrodden and disadvantaged he had somehow forgotten the forgotten American Indian:

But when Marion talked of her work she could turn him on. Her account of the life on the reservation in Jemez Springs in New Mexico was particularly moving, a place where the living standard of the thousand Navahos was so low, where until 1974 all the school children in the first six grades had to share one classroom. . . .

Yet ironically her zeal, her learning and convictions, her investigation of Jemez Springs which she would be resuming on her return—all this also told him what he didn't want to know: that there was small chance of ever holding her here or getting her back to Monaco on a permanent basis. But the final irony was of his own making: he was the one who was rooted now; he was the one who had turned in his passport. . . .

They'd rested there in silence and the room was veiled in smoke and he saw how she was once again studying the wall across from the bed, the north wall, a black-and-white explosion of newsprint—that collage he'd started one drunken night and to which he kept adding from time to time until it had become like an abstract painting, like an early Rauschenberg: all these newspaper clippings, headlines, lead stories, wire photos; all these fragments he'd cut out and pasted up: the carnage of the "Vietnam peace"; Nixon's vows of Watergate innocence; assassins trying to gun down clean-cut, honest Jerry Ford, baby; photographs of vials of poisonous toxins the CIA had kept on ice to eliminate foes of "national security." (The last time Eileen Blake of GYP had been in this bed it had been definitely for the last time; she had finally voiced her disapproval of his collage; it offended her: she was, after all, an overseas American in good Republican standing. Nick was offended, too, not by her being a Republican but because of the reasons that had made her and some others like her such dragass conservatives, the mistaken notion that since so many esteemed members of the rich or social class were traditionally Republican, she too, by sharing their labels and slogans, might somehow graft onto herself their kind of identity, image. Fare thee well, Eileen, my belle.)

For a while they talked about Sheldon Bradley and the way he'd behaved after Nick had danced with Simona. And Sheldon not even saying good night to Nick. It was the first time he'd ever seen Sheldon show his insides.

Marion put out her cigarette and went into the bathroom and when she came back she began brushing her hair:

Again the similarities with Jane. The absent way she tilted her head while she brushed away; the long torso, certain inflections of certain words. And she had that same private way of eyeing him: for like Jane she understood his weaknesses, his tics, his particular virtues. . . .

He thought of Jane, yes. But now the pain was less acute. Marion seemed to perceive this. When she got back into bed, she said:

"Were you thinking of her just now, Nick? There was something on your face, a look, and—"

"No—well, yes and no. It's something that I can't quite put together."

"What?"

"I don't know how to explain it, it sounds nutty, but I have these guilt feelings about the way I feel about you, about us. I never thought I'd ever find again what I had with Jane, never feel this way about anyone again. But now with you—" Nick sat up in bed. He had to try to convey his conflicting feelings: having for so long made a sacred memory of Jane he felt somehow guilty in having an experience with Marion that was as fine or beautiful as the first one had been. But in talking about it with Marion he came on an aspect he hadn't thought of before. "Maybe," Nick said, "it's the first experience that gives the second one its edge, its fullness."

"I've never had a second one." Marion's level gaze was on him. "I wonder—oh, I don't know—maybe, Nick, what I think you ought to think is to separate Jane from everything else. I mean, if that was so great, keep it great. But separate. And special." She kept biting on her lower lip. "I mean, the way you feel about me, what we have together, that's also great, isn't it? Also special. But completely separate, different. It's not supposed to be a repeat. It shouldn't be a re-run or a rip-off."

"I know that. That's part of the trouble. But there are these—these incredible similarities between you and Jane. It isn't Jane I want again. It's you. I know it, and I know that's why I'm sitting on all this guilt, as if I've been kidding myself all this time, telling myself it would never happen again, and now it's happened." He turned to her. "Do you have to get back next Tuesday?"

"Yes."

"Can't you put it off?"

"No way, Nick."

"You can finish all the work right here. In my

apartment. And I can get you a good typist. That'll give us at least another week or two. Christ, Marion, I—"

"I couldn't, it wouldn't work for me, Nick. I have to be back *there*. It's all in New Mexico, it's not here. . . . Besides, this material is much too tricky to trust to any people here. I have it all set up back home and it's got to be done without a single error. . . . I mean, after all my work, I can't submit this paper to U.S.C. unless it's as perfect as I can get it. Nick, this project, it's everything I've been into for the past three years. It's everything—"

"What about afterward?" He'd been wanting to ask her for days.

"What do you mean?"

"If you make it at U.S.C. Then what? Do you stay put?"

"Yes."

"How put? You wouldn't consider swapping it for —let's say, coming back over here? With me?"

"Oh, Nick—how could I? Not here. Ever. I don't understand how *you* can stay on. I'm not even sure you know yourself."

He looked at her. "When I came here it was to get away, not just from myself, but everything else back there and all the bad trips I'd been on. I guess this place has sort of become my private island. It has nothing to recommend it, except . . . no violence, no killing. You don't have to put four locks on the door. I can live better and work less and what I earn I keep. I don't have to support any cause I don't believe in, I don't have to—" He stopped; he was beginning to sound too defensive. And maybe he was. "What I'm trying to say, Marion, is that, sure, this place is . . . it's bullshit but it's benign. Back home, well . . . "

"It's different with me, though. My old beliefs are still intact. Or almost."

"Look, Marion, I'm not going to hassle you on that. All I know is what you mean to me and all I want to know is what the hell are we going to do?"

She shook her head. She sat up and put her arms around him. "Couldn't you come to California if it works out for me there?" The simple question emerged more like a plea.

"Marion, I told you. I can't live in the U.S.A. again. Oh, Christ, why did you have to show up here—"

"Thank God I did."

"Thank him for what? For bringing you? Giving me back what I wrote off for all time?"

"Nick, no one can stop you from coming to California. At least for a while."

"And see you when? Between classes?"

"How would you want it?"

"The way I want it, baby, is I want to live with you all the time, not just visit you. I don't want to be the pause that refreshes between classes and papers and faculty meetings. I love you, Marion, and I also happen to love what you stand for. And if you gave all that up for me I'd have to be hating myself right around the clock."

"What's the answer, Nick?"

"The answer is we'd end up hating each other

because my answer wouldn't work out."

Very quietly, too quietly, as she regarded his wall collage, Marion said, "Maybe your answer is still copping out. Are you?"

Nick started to reply, bombast hovered on his lips. But he realized he was unable to summon any reply that would satisfy her or his own deepest self:

In a spasm of self-reproach or disgust or hopelessness, he suddenly got out of bed and began to tear at the fragments of newsclippings on the wall as if the answers he'd been so desperate to discover were beneath the newsprint, buried, obscured by the floral wallpaper. . . .

"Nick—" Marion came to his side, she grasped his hand. "Nick, stop it! I'm sorry. I—"

He stopped, he looked at her. But then he turned, shaking, and stared back at the now scarred wall—all those scissored news clippings, his epitaphs for a place he would never see again.

The low ring of the telephone startled him like the sudden shrill of a fire siren.

"Yes?" At this late hour it had to be anything but good.

"Nick—" It was Simona, her breath was harsh, rapid, as if she'd been running uphill: could he please help her?

Now! Right away! A doctor. Ambulance. It's Sheldon. Unconscious. "Hello—Nick, Nick, can you hear me . . . ?"

14

To hear Sheldon, hear him talking to the nurse in an almost civilized way was to Simona the first positive sign that he was beyond danger.

And she had a spasm of remorse for having prematurely sent for his son; she might have waited but the heart specialist, an arch alarmist, had insisted she notify next-of-kin.

Sheldon, even after he began to respond to treatment, wondered if he'd survive. All his life he'd lived with a deep fear of hospitals; thankfully he'd been unconscious in the ambulance — he'd dreaded ambulances maybe even more than hospitals. As for nurses and technicians touching his person or assisting him to pee in a bedpan or bathing his private parts — he damn near had a relapse resisting these daily ministrations. . . .

She had had to send for his son. No choice. The

doctor had not minced words: he had prepared her for the worst.

So that she called Sheldon's former partner in New York and it took several days before he could locate the son in Los Angeles: Sheldon Junior was due in M.C. today or tomorrow. And Simona dreaded the prospect, knowing Sheldon's feelings.

This had been without doubt the darkest week in her life — frantic days and nights, shattered nerves, hysteria and sleeplessness. She had also lost five pounds, bringing her back to the size six and a flat hundred and ten pounds, the same as she was when she'd first met Nick, sassy and slim-assed, out of Texas.

But Sheldon was convalescing with a speed that almost gave Simona back the faith she'd been brought up with: when she'd prayed, when she'd actually heard herself pleading with a God in whose existence she'd stopped believing at the age of fourteen — then she knew how desperate she was. And she still continued to pray in gratitude for the way Sheldon was beginning to come back to life.

The night of the heart attack she had covered him with her old blue-and-white-striped terrycloth bathrobe as they lifted him onto the stretcher and into the ambulance. This morning, however, he requested the hotel send over his silk dressing gown, his monogrammed pajamas and his toilet articles. She joked about this, saying, "I'm sure, Sheldon, if you'd had your way, you would have had your own monogrammed oxygen tent."

In illness he was certainly the opposite of Simona. Whenever she was sick she would go into solitary, she couldn't bear the sight or sound of anyone. Sheldon, though still uncomfortable, wanted friends, he even insisted that there be a complete assortment of booze on hand for any visitors and "for my own morale."

Visitors had not been permitted until this afternoon, and Marie McFarland was the first one to come over (John was away on business, this time in Iran). Marie brought Sheldon the illustrated biography of Balzac by V.S. Pritchett. And Sheldon was so delighted he kept her in the room five minutes after the nurse firmly announced the time was up. The time was more than up. For almost immediately his eyes were closing in sleep.

Simona accompanied Marie McFarland downstairs to the entrance lobby of the hospital. As they said goodbye Simona saw a young man, holding a PanAm bag, at the reception desk. He was asking the girl to "ring Mr. Bradley's room."

"Who's calling?" the receptionist asked.

"Sam Bernstein. Sam Bernstein, *Junior.*"

Simona had no way of knowing who this was. She'd never seen him before. But it came back to her now that the only time Sheldon had ever discussed his son he had referred to him as Junior.

Obviously no connection. Even so, she found herself going over to the young man and asking if perhaps he was a friend of Sheldon's.

"His son," Sam Bernstein, Junior answered.

She stared at him as if to challenge his preposterous statement.

"Family name," he said immediately. "Had it changed last February. I was going to have cards printed up and send one to him. How is he?"

"Better ... much better ... when I sent for you, the doctor thought he wouldn't—" Simona was trying to be brisk, as natural as possible. She couldn't show what she was feeling, the chaos inside her — not because of what she had just learned, that didn't disturb her, and possibly it didn't even surprise her.

Yet looking at this young man, at his incredible dissimilarity to Sheldon, ungainly, prematurely thinning hair, unyouthful promise of belly — all this troubled her only because she was seeing him through Sheldon's eyes.

And she knew she had to keep the son away from the father.

Oh, shit! Why had she listened to that dismal poop of a doctor! Why? Because she had been too hysterical to do anything else, too dependent on him. . . .

Sam Bernstein.

"He's under heavy sedation," she improvised now. "He can't have any visitors." Then: "You see, at first, they thought he wouldn't make it. That's why I sent for you."

"Well, I'm here. And if I can't see the sonofabitch, that's okay with me. I only came over because I thought I'd have to be here to inherit some bread. I could use it."

Bravado? His coming on that strong—it could have been bravado. Or a terrific built-in self-protectiveness: for he blinked and his fingers kept working:

Ohchrist, even knowing this was Sheldon's son, she could scarcely believe it. What a cruel trick fate had played on Sheldon.

Still, the way he stood there, restive, uncertain, his hostility lost some of its force and Simona found herself feeling a kind of pity for him:

If she could divert him, get him out of the hospital . . . she suggested—and she knew even as she spoke that she was making a mistake—she suggested that if he wished he could stay at her house.

That was all right with him.

She could drive him up there now.

Sure.

And she would be happy to have him join her for dinner.

But he seemed to hesitate, falter. He looked around. He shifted his weight. Okay . . . maybe since he couldn't see the old man, maybe he could get a look at Monte Carlo, case the place, kill some time. . . .

Of course.

If only Nick were here now. Nick would have taken care of him.

But no. No, it wouldn't have worked: For Sheldon's sake she had to keep the boy under wraps. Somehow.

Simona was in no state to give him one of those Nick tour-bus spectaculars. But she went through the motions; she had to. After all, who had sent for him?

Who had done the right thing? Who wanted to do the right thing? That's right: your very own little dumb-ass Simona (who, much like young Sam Bernstein, had also been sort of unwanted; when she was born she turned out to be a real sure-enough girl, and disappointed daddy-dear had to add the *A* to her name to give rich Uncle Simon the butterfinger of posterity; except childless rich Uncle Simon didn't buy it; when he died all he left daddy-dear was grandpa's ancient gold timepiece, which finally came her way after daddy's humble estate was settled . . .).

She pointed out the Monaco landmarks, the palace, the church where that famous wedding had taken place, the harbor, the fabled Casino, the gardens — "some of those palm trees," she heard herself spiel, "were planted by the Phoenicians more than two thousand years ago."

"Yeah?" He muttered something about California — this place sort of reminded him of Southern California. "I have to be back there no later than a week from yesterday."

"That soon?" she felt obliged to ask.

"They only gave me seven days."

"Who?"

"Parole Board."

Simona gripped the wheel. "Parole Board?"

"Yeah. Better not tell that to the old man."

She waited. Nothing more. God. Just as well. In total silence they passed that piece of modern Danish pastry, the Sporting Club, then passed the Beach

Club and drove up the hills to her house. She gave
him a hasty tour of her place and only after he'd had
two drinks — he liked rum and coke, and she'd put
away a double martini — she asked him what had
happened. "Please tell me, Sheldon—I mean—"

"*Sam.*"

"Yes, of course. What happened, Sam?"

"No big deal. I needed money."

"But I thought your father—"

"Sonofabitch lays five hundred on me every
month. But I always run short. Five hundred. Payoff.
To keep me out of sight."

Simona reached for words. She wanted to encour-
age him to go on, to let it out. But he was so cool. As
if he'd been saying all this for years. Which he
probably had.

Finally he continued. "Needed the bread. All I did
was put my hands on three hot new films and made
some prints and sold them to foreign film dis-
tributors. Sure, I transferred some company checks
into my own account and almost made it. But that
bookkeeper got on to it and ran to the police. I got
off, though. The boss got me off. Still can't figure out
why or how. But he did. Now I'm on parole. A real
drag. Like being back in some stupid school." He
had been moving nervously around the living room.
He handed her his empty glass and dropped into the
easy chair. "Hey, this is neat here. I dig this place.
Like a real home, you know . . . ?"

Surely—she was embarrassed by this spontaneous

outburst—surely—no, that was not it. . . . She had to be careful, she had to lead him back, back to the beginning. She wouldn't be able to understand anything until she learned, until she found out . . . Surely, she said, he'd grown up in a home just as "neat," just as "real."

"Bull. I didn't grow up. I grew down. My old man . . . our house was more like those museum exhibition rooms. But boy, do I still hear him. Wash your hands, Sheldon. Stand up straight, Sheldon. Don't lean against the wall, Sheldon. Lower your voice, Sheldon. Sheldon, my ass! And he sent me to the fanciest private Catholic boys' school money could buy. Felt right at home there. Especially after my mother told me the truth. And some of the boys in school started to call me a — aw, forget it. I don't know what kind of crap he's been feeding you — I don't care. All I know, I had it up to here by the time I could lift a baseball bat." He passed a belligerent hand across his throat. "You know, I can't remember my father ever going anywhere with me? Never played ball with me, never came to the park with me, never came to those stupid school plays. Sure he was busy. But how come all the other fathers found time for their kids?"

Uncomfortably, as this portrait of her lover was being sketched in, she lit another cigarette. God, she had to cut down, smoking like a chimney since Sheldon's heart attack, and now even more. She put the cigarette out and fixed more drinks. It gave her something to do. It filled the void of sudden quiet.

What could she do? Say? Did she really have to listen to all of this? Did she really want to know all of it? Did she really care that much? This late? She'd never had a child. How could she judge anything? Understand any of this?

Slowly, very slowly, he turned around and stared at her. Kept staring at her. His eyes searched hers. Searching for what? For the reason his father loved her? To find out how she could love his father? Well, she could tell him that, all right. Oh shit, cut it out! She reached for his glass and handed it to him. Without a word he settled himself on the sofa, slumped into it, put his feet on the coffee table. He took a deep gulp, and then: "Here's to you, Simona. You're okay. Or do you want to hear more? Hell no. Don't blame you."

Oh, God, if she could only have vanished, disappeared. If she could have said get lost. But that was exactly what Sheldon had always told him.

The phone. Oh, God, thank you! The telephone. No matter who or what.

Sheldon's voice. He'd slept two hours, the doctor had been in. And now he was reading. What was she doing?

Nothing special. A drink and shortly dinner.

She tried to control her voice, keep the conversation natural, neutral. Let Sheldon do the talking.

"That book Marie brought, exactly right for my mood. And so beautiful to look at. I've got to send her a note—"

"Yes, do that."

"Simona."

"Yes?"

"If I ever doubted your love—What time will you be here tomorrow?"

"Same time."

Junior's brooding eyes were on her. "You didn't tell him I was here."

No. She couldn't. Not now. No surprises for Sheldon. Much too dangerous.

"Yeah. Well, I wouldn't want the sonofabitch to pass out just because I came all the way over here to see him."

"He can't have any emotional—"

"Yeah. I dig."

She was surprised to see that his glass was almost empty. "Let me get you a refill."

"Thanks. Hey, you're going to spoil me." He followed her over to the cabinet. (Just a little over a week ago Sheldon had stood here going through his unchanging ritual of fixing their martinis; those perfect and wonderful afternoons which, in his way, he could turn into daily celebrations. And ohgod, how she regretted the way she'd put him down, how she'd refused to accept him totally, or to marry him: if she'd known what was ahead she would have rushed him to the nearest judge or priest — or . . . no, no rabbi for Sheldon.)

Sam tasted the fresh drink. "You're going to spoil me, Simona," he said again. "Hey — " He sniffed.

"That smells great. What's cooking? Smells like chili."

"It is." She had frozen a big batch and earlier tonight had popped it into the oven. She always kept it on hand. For her own occasional pleasure. Sheldon called them "these little Texas ulcer festivals of yours."

"Yeah, that sounds like him all right." Then: "What I want to know is what did he do to rate someone like you, Simona? What the hell do you see in him? His money? Naw. I'm sorry. Hell, that's stupid. I'm always meeting some guy who's nowhere and then I meet his girl or his wife and she's great." A pause, and then: "Never happens to me."

"What doesn't?"

"Meeting someone great."

"You will."

"Yeah, sure. You're an optimist, the sunshine type. Yeah, but I almost did. Last Christmas. I met this girl. Linda. She was — you know, like wow! But I blew it!"

He blew it, he admitted, almost eager to let it all come out. He ruined it because he ended up in jail and who the hell could blame her for dusting him off after that.

Maybe, Simona attempted to soothe him, maybe when he returned to California, Linda would have changed her mind.

"Naw. No way. I called her before I came over

here, told her my old man was dying. But you know, she didn't even hear me out, she just hung up." Then: "I'd say the cards are stacked, somebody is fixing the deck—" A sudden outburst: "Your friend, my father, that sonofabitch—"

Simona wanted to close her ears and her eyes. She had to clear out of here. Leave him alone. Her nerves were raw. No more, please! But how could she clear out? Isn't that what Sheldon had done . . .

"What about your mother, Sam? Are you—"

He cut her off. "Leave her out of this. She tried. And how she tried. But he never listened to her. It had to be the de Rham dancing school, all those little society creeps I had to cha-cha with. Except that those nice little girls didn't cha-cha with me. They just said, 'Hi, repulsive' and kept going. My mother finally yanked me out of there. Took me to the psychiatrist. But after the divorce, after she and I moved out west, we had a good time together. She was great. Really. For six months. Then she met this guy and married him and he's just like my old man. That's when I pulled out. . . . "

Simona was living all of it. And she fervently wished she could say something, do something. But she felt so goddam helpless.

"That chili is about ready, Sam."

She served it on the coffee table, along with a bowl of salad and beer.

For a while it looked as if he had calmed down, lost his belligerence. He consumed the chili with an almost animal ferocity. And after dinner she showed him her workroom. She told him how she too had bailed out of her home and hometown . . . how she'd gone alone, with no good-luck blessings from her father, who'd always seemed to resent her presence in the world merely because she wasn't born with a penis. As for her mother, she'd been stricken with polio a year after Simona'd been born and been confined to a wheelchair until her death ten years later. . . .

It had all given her, she supposed, a fierce determination to embrace life as fully as she could, to live with gaiety, to open herself to experience: and experience meant going to New York. A week after she'd graduated from the University of Texas she went east. . . .

"And that's when I ran into all the grief. At first. I mean, the jobs I wanted didn't want me. Or when they did, they didn't work out. Everything went wrong and of course I blamed it all on my parents. It gave me a terrific excuse for feeling sorry for myself. Then I met a guy called Nicholson, Harper Nicholson. I had a big crush on him. And one day after I'd bad-mouthed my daddy for everything from my big feet to my small breasts, Nick looked at me and said he was fed up with all the kids who used their parents like crutches. He said everybody had a long list of gripes against daddy and mommy but they mostly used it to alibi their own shortcomings and failures. You just have to make it on your own. Make it with what you've got, he said. You know, Nick was right. I did learn to live with myself and make it myself. . . ."

She waited, she watched his face. But there was no way of knowing if she'd reached him, if she'd gotten through to him.

Sam picked up the gold pin Simona was currently working on. "I used to know a girl. She made jewelry too. But only copper or silver. Not gold like you. She was great. I really liked her. But she—she just took off with this creep." He put down the pin, picked up a pair of pliers, clicked them open and shut. Then: "You know, that's what spooks me. My great father, can't use his real name. Why not? Bernstein. What's wrong with Bernstein? Leonard Bernstein conducts symphonies. Bernstein what's-his-name, wrote that book on Watergate. A bestseller. Ginsberg. Another Jew? No, that's not what people think of when they hear that name. They know he's a poet. And even movie stars—but my father—"

"Your father — " Simona interrupted the litany. "He's a different generation, Sam. When he was a boy—in those days being a Jew could be rough. Very rough, Sam. Nobody can blame your father for having changed his name. Jews did it in those days. Now it's different. No one cares now. It's even kind of an exotic asset. But when he was young he was up against real anti-Semitism. You also have to understand that in those days no one understood your father or how he felt. And I have to understand that, too, Sam."

"Yeah, well, that's his funeral. Why did he have to lay his grief on me? He thinks by buying me off he comes out the number one WASP? He always buys me off. Once I opened a little restaurant in Venice—California. I couldn't quite handle it. When it bombed he bailed me out. But you should have heard him! A cheap, junky restaurant! *His* son! All I tried was trying to make a living. I told myself screw him. So I went into business with another guy. We opened a 'Photographic Studio'—you know, you rent the camera and take pictures of live models. Strictly for jerkoffs, freaks. But at least we did a hell of a business. Made real money. On Melrose Avenue in Hollywood. My partner was a good guy. But he flips out for one of our models and they both disappear. With all the cash. But this time I didn't call the old man. I answered an ad and got myself a job with this film distributor, the best on the coast. I thought I had it made. But then—well, you know the rest. Forget it."

"Sam — " She put her arm across his shoulder. "We've all been through bad scenes. I told you before, I'm no exception. But, Sam, you're still so young, you have so much time ahead of you, you—" Oh, God, what other banalities could she come up with?

"Sam, listen to me. You've got to stop looking back.

You've got to look ahead. It'll be different now. Sheldon will change. You know he was near death, and when you've been close to death you change a lot of your thinking—"

As if he had not been listening to her at all, he said: "How does he rate someone like you? He's never had to sweat it out. He was born lucky and he gets away with all of it. He'd kill me if he could." Then: "Maybe I'll do him a favor and save him the trouble." He looked away. "Forget it, Simona. I'm sorry. I'm a stupid drag. I've always been a drag."

He turned, hurried away from her and into the spare room. She started after him, but stopped herself. She lit a cigarette and her hands were unsteady: it had been too much. He'd put too much on her and maybe she had put too much on him. But she had had to, she had had to try and reach him, get through to him, break down the walls of his pride, hostility. . . .

She glanced toward the back room: Surely he'd pull himself together. By morning he'd be all right and they'd have breakfast and they'd be able to talk more rationally. She would be able to help him, and when he'd be back home she would call him once a month or he would be able to call her whenever he felt the need for someone to talk to. . . .

She was exhausted. Drained. She took a hot, steaming bath. Always had eased her nerves, her tensions. Always made her sleep. But it didn't work. Sleep did not come. She couldn't stop thinking, worrying about him. And she kept seeing Sheldon in the trauma of his fatherhood. . . .

She did not know how long she had been lying there, wretched and filled with an unholy sense of helplessness: ohgod, please let me sleep.

She stiffened in her bed. Those sounds. Or had she dozed off, had she dreamt it — no. She listened. Sounds from the back room. She felt paralyzed with fear: his muttering of suicide. But she couldn't take that seriously. She refused to take that seriously. And anger replaced her fears. She felt annoyed and impatient with him for having become so maudlin, for having used that melodramatic ploy for pity. . . .

But the sounds grew louder, more terrifying. She went barefoot, in her nightgown, to the spare room. She stopped in front of the door:

Sobbing. Muffled, terrible. She had to go in:

The room was bright with the summer's night. And she saw that his whole body was shaking.

"Sam, please, Sam, what is it? Sam, please tell me."

He kept his head turned to the wall. Moonlight illumined his convulsed body. She walked over to the window and drew the curtains, then sat down on the bed.

Abruptly he twisted himself around, groped for her hands.

Oh god! She pressed his fingers. She couldn't talk. She didn't know what to say. What was there to say? She wasn't even sure how or what she felt. Anger? Pity? No: what she felt, what she knew, was how desperately he needed acceptance, human acceptance. . . .

The sobbing subsided. He stirred. His cheek was against her cheek and her cheek was wet with his tears:

Slowly she recognized what he had to have. She let him hold her. He tightened his hold as if he was afraid she might leave him, escape, reject him. The way everyone else had . . .

His breathing became strident. He nuzzled his face into the side of her throat, as if seeking protection or warmth. His mouth sought more, his mouth on her flesh. Like a child.

She could not move. It would have been cruel.

Abruptly his hands were grasping her, all over her, reaching down, pleading between her legs. And arched up against her there was the sudden fierce pleading of his erection:

Demanding. Crying out for closeness, acceptance. Pleading for recognition of his existence. Or maybe even a final vengeful act of triumph over his father. . .

"Simona. Please."

"No."

"Please. Simona."

"Sam. No!"

She was rigid, frozen, enraged, frightened. And all the time she knew that his almost brutal insistence was beyond ordinary lust:

She recognized the nature of his demand but that didn't help. She understood but she couldn't in any way yield to it, to him. He overpowered her with a lifetime of harnessed hostility. Unceasingly, he kept forcing that same brutal demand on her and there was no way to escape, not now. His weight, his need, crushed her and he went into her, full into her, crying out now—a boy's cry. Helpless. Or a plea. For love? Mercy? Revenge? Or the womb's safe darkness?

PART IV *October*

Like most of the Americans here, I missed the falling leaves, the fragrant announcement of autumn. Yet a fine October freshness wafted in from the sea, and the sun put a diamond dazzle on the early snow cresting the lower Alps.

By now all of the jazzy international gang, the social Mafia, had jetted or sailed off and the residents of Monaco were reclaiming their territory.

The beginning of October, however, brought charter-plane loads of off-season, off-price conventions to Loew's Monte Carlo Hotel (tourist groups at bargain prices were, of course, never permitted at the Hotel de Paris) and the principality exploded with open faces and drip-dry plaid pants: the streets, the shops, the Casino, the Oceanographic Museum, the Botanical Garden and the palace square were invaded, and the twang of middle America fell with

217

a kind of sweet brashness on the soft immemorial Mediterranean air. . . .

I remember seeing Sheldon Bradley, a week after he'd been released from the hospital, waiting for a taxi outside the Residence du Parc — the doctor would not yet allow him to drive — and though he was thinner he looked resplendent in classic tweed jacket and flannels; like most people reprieved from death the simplest joys of living marked his features: his gray eyes, his quiet voice, were alive with new vigor: he and Simona were spending much of their time preparing the apartment. He was having the third bedroom converted into a workshop for her; the alterations, decorating and the arrival from New York of his choicest antiques — all this was being coordinated so that the apartment would be ready for occupancy and for their marriage. Sheldon, the penultimate ritualist, couldn't get married just any place or any time: and I suspected that with Simona's flair and his panache, their wedding party would be considerably more than a mundane date on the social calendar of Monte Carlo.

As for Nick, he wasn't around as much these days and the bar of the hotel looked almost unfriendly and unfamiliar without the familiar fair-haired figure who had made it his office for so long. True, he had ended a moderately profitable season with that handsome commission on the sale of Alma Ainsworth's apartment, and his finances were certainly at a new high. Yet he did not seem at his best: he wasn't quite as gregarious. He seemed more withdrawn. . . .

I recall leaving the Tennis Club late one morning when Nick arrived with McFarland; he and the arms trader often played tennis together but stayed away from the courts during the crowded hot summer months. On this sunny morning I joked with Nick about his not working and having joined the idle rich; but he said "so far as hustling real estate, I just can't get it together right now."

What about that trip to New Mexico he'd mentioned a few weeks ago? He'd cancelled it. Since then he'd planned another trip to the States for a month, but now, that too, was definitely out.

"Couldn't get a visitor's visa. Not yet." Nick kept fingering his racquet. "I'm number one on their shitlist."

Why someone with Nick's principles would spend time with McFarland always had troubled me. But I believed I understood it now. It was his way of showing appreciation for the way John had often befriended him, vouched for him, and always would. As for our "friendly neighborhood merchant of death," it was very difficult for him to find tennis partners: who else but Nick would tolerate McFarland's unpredictable moods? Who else but Nick would tolerate those manners of his: the way, if he flubbed a backhand shot, he would hurl his racquet against the high wire fence; or if he sent his serve into the net, losing game point, he would fling the racquet, cracking it onto the clay, and emit a verbal volley of crudest slang, emphasizing sexual organs and bowel functions regardless of who might be on the adjacent courts.

On this day I saw McFarland was using tennis as a therapeutic diversion. Ever since he learned the African Defence Minister's return to Monte Carlo was being delayed for two weeks, McFarland seemed more erratic, overtly nervous. I would not have liked to be in Marie's place during this period, but she was a woman who—

"All right, my friends"—the arms dealer swung his racquet in a swift, almost vicious forehand stroke—"do we stand here chit-chatting or do we play? Jesus almighty, Nicky, you look like a member of parliament who just got voted out. Let's fuck off, chaps, and play some tennis."

This was the last time I saw McFarland and Nick alone together. For after the African Defence Minister came back to Monte Carlo the life of each person in the group was shatteringly altered.

And even, to some extent, my own: for though I had planned to return to New York to coordinate all the work, the writing I'd done on tax shelters from the Bahamas to Luxembourg, Switzerland and Monaco, I decided to defer this project and stay on where I was:

I decided to settle down and attempt to record and interpret all the experiences, relationships, personalities and events I'd observed, or become immersed in so innocently from almost the first day I'd come to Monte Carlo. So that, I hoped, all I had seen in the beginning I would be able to witness or learn about straight through to the end.

15

The taxicab, a Mercedes of the same model Sheldon had owned in New York, drove hillward above Monte Carlo. The afternoon was a bit raw; it was always chilly up here, the sun filtering coolly, greenly through the pines. . . .

He would build a fire.

Ah, how grand to see her house these days! Since the hospital he'd had this new regard for it. On the August night when he'd blacked out he knew, or feared, even as he lost consciousness, that he would never see it again. . . .

There was a fire going, that is, it was just beginning to flicker; Simona must have lit it as soon as she'd heard the taxi: another touch to spare the patient any strain? He appreciated it. Yet he didn't.

He mustn't. That was the order of the day. Doctor's orders.

Cocktails? Only one. *He mustn't* have more.
Sex? He *mustn't* overdo it. Or better none at all.
Worry? *He mustn't*. Under any condition.

Not even if it was about the half-million dollars he had out on loan. McFarland's generous promise of that high interest in no way seemed to lessen his anxieties. For suddenly all of John McFarland's anxieties were his too: there had been this prolonged delay in Kuandi's return and John had been just a bit too reassuring about it for comfort. . . .

No worries: but Sheldon couldn't stop thinking of everything he shouldn't think of. His gourmet cravings were restricted, his drinking was restricted; no cigarettes, not ever again. And broodingly, he always came back to sex.

But he couldn't let it. Other men had been through it. But few had had a Simona: when he thought of that endless siege in the hospital, the way Simona had taken over, the way she had managed. Night and day. No rest and almost no sleep, on hand all the time, alert for any error or negligence, catering to his needs . . .

Her attentions, her devotion—how could he ever have doubted her feelings for him? How could he have brooded about her and Nick? . . .

During those long tedious twilights when boredom or the spectres of his health haunted him, she'd gotten him through, sitting beside him on his bed and reading out loud from magazines or books an hour or two or sometimes until she'd become so hoarse he would insist she stop. . . .

He had had to go through all this anguish to discover the unspoken depths of the love beneath her love.

During the years of his outstanding career in New York, he thought now, could he look back and honestly say he had had a single true friend?

His own business partner, Howard Mitchell—even Howard was a man he would never have turned to for help. . . .

Much of it had been his own fault: he'd been too concerned with Sheldon Bradley, with his own upward mobility and acquiring all the symbols of esteem he needed at any cost, at anybody's cost. . . . When you dedicated your life to yourself, you had to expect to end up standing alone. Or sleeping or dying alone . . .

Whenever he tried to review his life, as he had during his siege in the hospital, he couldn't comprehend why it eluded him. Why, unlike most people, was he unable to recapture his past? But he realized, or admitted finally, that he couldn't see or feel himself or be a part of his own past: the real and the synthetic had merged, leaving recollections that were vague, unreliable, untrue. His past was part of a long charade, year after year, a profitable, rewarding, flattering charade, a game he'd always kept winning.

But a game.

So that now all his deceptions with a person of Simona's honesty were beginning to rise up in him and he was beginning to taste the bile of his own counterfeit life.

And still, after all that had happened between them he still lacked the courage, the guts to meet the truths of her life with the truths of his own.

Simona greeted him at the door, her arms were around him and he was again aware of an ineffable difference, an edge of tenderness that had come into being since his illness.

They were kissing: her tongue played against his. *He mustn't.* He said: "My kingdom for a drink."

"Shall I fix them?"

"You? Since when?" He consulted his watch. "Twenty more minutes."

"Oh, to hell with it, Sheldon. If we want a drink let's have it—never mind, I know you. You'd rather wait and anticipate."

He deposited the book of fabric swatches he'd brought with him onto the old refectory table behind the sofa.

"If it wasn't for you, Sheldon," she'd said the day when they were at the greenhouse buying plants for the apartment terrace, "I'd never move. Not that I'm complaining about the Residence du Parc."

"Well, we all have our crosses to bear." He had teased her.

"Oh, I love you!" She'd embraced him amid the jungle of ferns.

But without a doubt, there was a difference these days. He wasn't sure if he liked it or not, this new margin of tenderness; at times it made him feel an invalid. Pampering was welcome but not if it made you feel you were in an invisible wheelchair.

Simona was saying: "Do you suppose the Great Anticipator would fix us the drinks now so we can go through those swatches? I know you're saving them for the drinks."

His watch told him there were still a few minutes to go. But he would compromise. He'd been looking forward to this ritual all day.

"Hmm—" Simona held up her glass. "Nobody but nobody can put together a martini like you, lover." And she reached for his hand and pulled him down beside her on the sofa. "Now let's see—" And they started to go through the fabrics for the upholstery and drapery for his library-office.

"I'm not sure what I'm going to do in that so-called office. After all," he pondered, "we have to admit there isn't much I can do around here. In New York it would be different."

"Oh, come on, don't tell me you're thinking about New York at this point." She shuddered. "Gives me the willies just thinking about it. Or any other place for that matter. I never want to cross another ocean— no more traveling *pour moi,* baby. If I never see another airport or another Vuitton bag, it'll be too soon for me. But if you have any qualms about living here permanently — I mean if you're going to miss the New York scene—let's discuss it—"

"For godsakes, Simona, I was only thinking out-loud. I'm still fishing for something to do, some activity to interest, excite, me. It has nothing to do with New York, not really." He sipped his drink, he dwelled on this ambrosial sin. Then: "Big cities no longer tempt me. I'm still shocked by all the sense-less murders, killings — not just in New York, but everywhere. Hostages killed by guerrillas at the Rome airport, in a Brooklyn bank innocent bystand-ers killed in another shoot-out, and look at that car in London that was blown up — a minute later and Caroline Kennedy would have been in it. No matter where you go or what you happen to be doing, you can suddenly be the victim of this kind of criminal madness." After a pause: "Monte Carlo has its short-comings, it's confining as a gilded cage. But we're safe here."

"You're getting to sound like Nick."

"Except that Nick doesn't seem to be sounding off very much these days, does he? I assume it's—"

"Yes. Marion. Poor Nicky."

"He's not so poor now." Sheldon had left his smouldering jealousy in that hospital room: the close-ness of death had dwarfed the trivial giants of ordinary concerns. Regretfully he noted that his glass was empty. "A small dividend—do you think I—"

Simona shook her head. "That's out, darling."

"Yes, I know." A wry smile.

Simona started to reach for a cigarette but decided against it: for the patient's sake? She was saying, "What's so rough for Nick is that he's nowhere now. And the way he's lived with Jane's memory all these years. And now God knows how long he'll stew over Marion."

"What was she like? I mean Jane. Was she really all Nick seemed to think she was?"

"More. She was such a great gal: half real, half fantasy. She had everything, they both did." Simona yielded to the cigarette, and she exhaled the smoke in his direction for his vicarious pleasure, as he'd asked her to. "You know, even now, I can scarcely believe that it happened. Talk about criminal madness." A pause. Reflectively she added: "And then you take someone like Frederico — he just bounces through life and gets it all his own way."

"I suppose so...." At Alma Ainsworth's farewell party the night before she'd sailed from Cannes on the Italian liner for New York, Sheldon and Simona, like the other guests, had been surprised that Frederico was not present:

"He's in Italy" — Alma had spoken with her customary candor and pragmatism "insisted on visiting all those jolly, fat relatives and all their bambinos. At least that's his story, which I am only passing on because I'd rather not think otherwise. He's flying over next week. You know, he's such a child. But if I tried to spank him, I'm afraid I'd end up killing him."

But Frederico would not likely get back to New York that soon. For Nick had given Simona and Sheldon the facts of his recent history, and it was neither astonishing nor appalling. It was simply Frederico:

He had gone to the Milan car dealer to buy, with

Nick's side-commission on the apartment sale, the Dino '71 Ferrari. While he was there, "a very distinguished, silver-haired dude" was in the garage section of the car agency having a repair or adjustment attended to on his car, also a Ferrari, but a 1975 model:

The man saw Frederico and Frederico saw the man, and then they left the garage and walked together to The Galleria to enjoy an aperitif. Frederico never did buy the Dino. Instead, he took off in that powerhouse '75, his new friend letting him do the driving. To Rome. Where, according to Nick, "this dude has a triplex penthouse overlooking the entire Forum."

Sheldon was restive, he kept fingering his cigarette lighter. He had to keep busy, active, diverted. While Simona figured out the yardage of the fabric they'd both decided on, he went into her workshop to take the dimensions of her workbench, which would be transferred to the apartment. He was about to return to the living room when his attention was drawn to a single object, a thin gold chain . . .

Amid the unfinished bracelets and the almost finished pin she'd been working on, this chain . . .

He picked it up. It lay in his palm, he studied it:

Sheldon was stupefied. The small pendant hanging from the chain — the St. Christopher medal. He turned it over. The initials: S.B. He'd given it to his son on his seventh birthday.

It couldn't be the same one, there was no way that it could have been the same one:

He kept staring at it. He was incapable of moving. His hand was petrified.

"Sheldon—" She had come into the workroom.

He glanced up: "This chain, Simona—where did you get it?"

16

Simona was unprepared for the confrontation. Though she had known she would be telling him about his son, she also knew it would be necessary to wait.

But how stupid of her to have left that chain lying there. Now there could be no waiting. And now she would have to tell only part of the truth.

"He left it here, Sheldon. Your son. I had to send for him." She had to come out with it as rapidly as she could. "The doctor insisted. But you were out of danger by the time he got here and I—"

"He came here? You saw him?" Sheldon's gray eyes were motionless.

"I had no choice." She had to go through all of it, the meeting in the hospital lobby, the drive through

Monaco, the dinner and his staying at her house that night. She could not, of course, go beyond that. And she could not tell Sheldon, not yet, that his son had reverted to the family name. . . .

"Where is he now?"

"He's gone back. Look, Sheldon, I know how you feel about him but I'm glad I met him, it's—"

"When did he leave?"

It had been the day after. He'd been asleep when she left in the morning for the hospital, and when she got back the house was empty:

There'd been the chain. And a note.

What kind of note? Why did he leave that medal? Sheldon's voice was strained; his eyes fixed on her with an acute intensity as if he were less concerned with his own feelings than hers, searching her features for what she must have been thinking about his son, what he might have told her and what, now, she might be thinking of Sheldon. . . .

"The note. What did he say, Simona?"

The note and the chain had been left on her worktable. He had written that he wanted to give her something, that he didn't have anything except this old medal, and he wanted her to have it. With his "gratitude." Simona omitted the final line: "And in case the sonofabitch doesn't believe I came all the way over here to see him, you can show him this."

Anguish was carved on the ivory pallor of Sheldon's face.

Anguish was also carved on her soul: she had never missed a period; and now she was seven weeks late. . . .

Was this her reward for what amounted to a kind of rape, a rape she had allowed to happen?

If, after that one nightmare night of her misguided pity, she was actually pregnant—oh God, at this late stage of her life—she would have to have an abortion, and she would lose her sanity because she had no one to blame. Only herself.

There would be no options.

Unless the pregnancy appeared to be Sheldon's responsibility. But even for this disgusting deception time was against her . . . almost against her. . . . Sheldon had made love to her the day before his heart attack—but even so, it was too sickening to contemplate . . . .

She was conscious of the way he was standing there. So inert. Watching her as one watches a person for signs or symptoms of an illness or an aberration, and she again had to submerge the rage, the terror that had been burning in her for seven weeks.

She had to remember that at a time like this it was Sheldon's life that was on the line. She went to him and took the chain and medal from his hand. "Look, Sheldon, please believe me, I'm glad he came and that we could talk. We talked a lot. It helped."

"Helped?"

"It helped me understand you. That's what I'm trying to say. Your being a Jew—mygod, Sheldon, I

don't give a shit about that. But at least now I understand why you do. Or did. And that's exactly what I
tried to convey to your son. I mean, how different it
was when you were a kid — that's what we talked
about."

Sheldon seemed to hear but not quite grasp any of
it. "Did he—did he tell you what he's doing, where
he is—"

"No." She had to lie.

"Do you know he—my son—was arrested for a—
do you know he's on parole?"

"Sheldon, for godsakes, half the people I knew in
New York or in Dallas had kids who were in trouble
one way or another. At least he's not into drugs, he's
not addicted. And I can promise you—I think he'll
be all right. I feel that I helped him — helped him
understand what you're all about—and I think maybe
I helped him understand himself a little better, too."

Only this weighted stillness. He kept standing
there. He didn't move. Finally he cleared his throat.
But he didn't speak.

"What is it, lover? Tell me."

"Nothing."

"Sheldon, will you please believe me — none of
this—not your past, not your son—none of it bothers
me, none of it matters. . . . The only thing that counts,
that matters, is you. Us."

Numbness still seemed to hold him. But finally he
said: "You know, Simona, I never really gave a damn.
It was nobody's business but mine. None of it. But

since you, Simona, every lie — every evasion — has cut into me like — I could only keep it up because it had become a habit, a natural reflex."

He shrugged his shoulders, his searching eyes left her face for the first time, and then he turned around, left the room and walked out through the back of the house to the garden and beyond. From the window she watched him: his back to her, his head bent low, his hands pressed to his face, and she could tell from the way he moved now that he couldn't stop his tears.

She wanted to go to him. But she knew the moment was too private. What he was going through now had to be borne alone.

17

The long-time burden was gone. Or almost gone. He stood there in his dressing gown and looked out the high windows of the hotel sitting room: viewing the great palms, and the magnolia trees and the somber blue of the sea. It was a new experience:

He was glad he had been forced into the open with Simona. His gladness had kept him from sleeping half the night. It didn't matter. For this morning he was more rational, more balanced than he'd been yesterday when he'd come upon the medal and chain, when he had to learn all Simona knew about him — and about his son. Today he was convinced that her regard for him had not been marred or warped.

Besides, wasn't it Simona herself who had once shouted at him: "You're so goddam perfect. You're not real—"

235

Well, now he was real!

This new sense of himself was precious. Was this how criminals felt when they confessed? How homosexuals felt when they came out of the closet?

Whatever it was, he now knew Simona would not leave him. He would not lose her. Now she was part of him and part of his whole life, his entire past. But in this burst of relief he would not pause to question or probe all the developments that had led to this newly gained sense of reality. Not now. It was, after all, impossible to reassess a lifetime overnight.

Yet, for a moment now, he could already view his son with less rancor. For in truth, his son, for whatever reason, at least had made the effort, the trip, to be with his father at the end. Which was more than Sheldon had done when he'd received that call from Detroit, from the neighbor who told him his mother had died. Lily was dead. What about the funeral and the arrangements? Could Sheldon come at once?

No, Sheldon could not—he knew he could, he told himself he should. But he couldn't. He had never been to a funeral—he had always avoided what he called these barbaric rites. And the news of Lily's death and being unable to bring himself to go, to attend her funeral revived all his old anxieties, guilts, phobias; and he'd held the telephone in his hand, unspeaking, inarticulate. Until finally he was able to say he was not well, and he would ask Lennie Levine, who was a lawyer in Kent Hills, Michigan, to look after the arrangements. Sheldon would pay all the expenses. . . .

And that is how it had been left, and to this day he did not know where his mother's grave was. . . .

Mid-afternoon and he and Simona were in bed. It was the first time since before the hospital:

He was, in effect, celebrating the beginning of a new era. For both of them. Nakedly they were again together and to him it seemed more exciting, more beautiful, than it had been at its best. The only difference was that Simona was quiet, the small murmuring utterances were not heard. He didn't know why.

He was caressing her breasts, savoring her; he rejoiced in the rediscovery of her body. Her hand was lightly on him, gently stroking him until his erection began. And all these past weeks he had lived with fear that his illness had damaged his sexual power.

Soon he stirred, turned, to lie sidewise, to face her, and to go into her. But she didn't let him. Instead, she raised herself and then he found her lying on top of him:

"Let her sit on it, let her do all the work," the cardiologist had warned both of them; the esteemed doctor could be relied on to crudely counsel them thus, not knowing how it offended Sheldon: let her do all the work. *Work!*

Simona was above him, her torso tapering above him, her thighs straddling him:

But slowly, abysmally, without warning, there was nothing for her to sit on:

And the more Simona moved, trying to resurrect him, the more impotent he became.

He sweated in panic.

He knew what had happened, suddenly knew:

The unwanted image of his son loomed between him and Simona: his son, whom she had seen and who had told her every unsavory detail he had secreted all his life. Yes. And even though she understood, even though she said it hadn't altered her feelings for him, he was convinced that their lovemaking was permanently flawed:

And now in the death of his erection, there was no way for him to consummate what should have been the glorious celebration of the life that had been restored to him.

Dismay, sorrow, like a cascade of regrets flooded through him as he saw her gently remove herself from his limp body. And where she had been there was now only the inhibiting image of his son.

No, Sheldon, no, she'd protested. It was nothing, it was to be expected. It was natural. It was just that everything at once—it would take time. . . .

Simona almost made him believe it. Almost . . .

He couldn't tolerate any more. He felt naked. He had to get away from here.

He went back to his hotel. He attempted to distract himself, defy his thoughts. He called Nick. But Nick didn't sound much livelier than Sheldon. Was Nick

free for dinner? Yes. How about a fine and proper
French dinner at the fine and proper restaurant, Le
Bec Rouge? Okay with Nick.

But conversation was sluggish with effort. Neither
of them was able to cheer the other. After dinner
Nick wanted to see the latest American film that was
playing tonight. Another one. Ironically, Nick
seemed to derive some sort of succor from these
films, and there were some American movies he had
even seen twice. . . .

For Sheldon, no such therapy. Not yet. Midnight.
He had taken a tranquilizer and now, belatedly, after
Simona's late telephone call—they had talked almost
half an hour—he began to absorb all she had been
trying to convey to him this afternoon and tonight:

All she had said, all she had told him, the passion
of her concern . . . all this was beginning again to
breathe new life and hope into his bruised psyche:

"Sheldon—" she had urged him, "you can't just
keep on living—you've got to *start* living!"

By morning, once again, he was Sheldon Bradley, the
euphoric, burdenless man.

But he must not dwell on himself. Activity. He had
to get over to the apartment. There was much he
wanted to attend to. He hadn't been there for the past
three days.

As he was leaving his suite, John McFarland called
him. Immediately, from the exuberant voice vibrat-

ing through the telephone, the familiar minstrel nonsense, he knew the arms trader had the best of news:

"Sheldon, my friend, I just wanted you to know, you've made a good investment. 'Tis of the very best. My black friend is here and there is the good green buck where his Oxonian mouth is. We're meeting at the bank and I would like to have your elegant ass right up here for lunch today. And it won't be chicken shit, it'll be chicken salad on your Sèvres plate. Compliments of the Godly gook you saved the night I needed to be saved. The portals of heaven will be wide open when you get there. Just as sure as the fires of hell will singe my balls even as I draw my last breath—"

One o'clock?

Right!

Right: A new day. All that anxiety had been in vain. His money would be returned. Plus.

And after the luncheon he would be going to Simona's. At three this afternoon. That's when she would be through with that gold pin she'd been hurrying to finish.

At three o'clock.

But today—or tomorrow, or—he would not try to make love to her.

There occurred to him now still another fear, another speculation: Had it actually been the vision of his son that had inhibited him yesterday? How could he be sure of what had caused that disaster? For all he knew he might have come out of the hospital an impotent man. Maybe it had nothing at all to do with his son:

Maybe it was himself. And if it was, God help him.

High in the Residence du Parc the work was progressing in his apartment: he stood in the open doorway watching the workmen, the painters — all these plain and busy men working with their hands: their minds, unlike Sheldon's, were not clogged by the sludge of sexual anxiety. And when they made love to their wives or girlfriends there was simple honest lust. To them Sheldon Bradley must seem the man with all the wealth and all the luck and all the women and all the . . .

The elevator door slid open: it was Marie McFarland. She waved to him, approached. Marie in pumpkin-colored skirt and matching sweater and her russet hair always with that sheen. "Oh, Sheldon — I'm so glad to find you here. I wanted to know if you've heard from John?"

Yes. He had.

"Oh, good. Then you're coming to lunch?" She peered inside. "I haven't seen this place in almost a month. May I come in?"

He led her into the immense white-walled living room. Beyond the closed sliding glass casements was the commodious terrace, the same size as the McFarlands' three floors above. His view was the same, a full one-hundred-and-eighty-degree sweep from the frontier of Italy to the Riviera peninsula of St. Jean Cap Ferrat.

He showed Marie through the apartment. The dining room, pantry, kitchen, the master bedroom. He took her to the north end, to his library-office; all the painting was done.

"Where is Simona's workshop going to be?" Marie inquired. Her scent, that perfume was heady, close, welcome: it helped to combat the acrid smell of the fresh paint.

Simona's workroom was at the east end, she needed morning sunlight, that's when she liked to work. From the windows you could see the roads that were cut into the mountainside.

They stepped into the room:

"Marie, watch it!" He warned her, but she stumbled, her right foot colliding with the haphazard, jagged pile of books on the floor. He managed to catch her, break her fall. "Sorry. Those books aren't supposed to be here. Are you all right?"

Uncertainly she nodded.

He braced her, held her, keeping her weight off her right side.

"Thank God you were quick, Sheldon. I know marble floors. They can be bone breakers."

"Are you sure you didn't break or twist anything?"

Her weight rested against him and he supported her as she bent down gingerly pressing, exploring her ankle and the instep. "I think — it's all right.

Thank you." Then a breathless stab at levity: "You see, Sheldon, you're being a perfect host even before you move in."

He continued to hold her: her perfume enshrouded them in an awkward intimacy.

Her face was near. Nearer now. Her mouth was closer. And their gazes were joined in that unmistakable instant of communication that hovered between them: that kind of precipitous instant people often experience just before a first kiss:

But neither of them broke the moment. And Sheldon was conscious of something else: his penis, inflamed, rigid.

There was another fraction of time, and then, as if by tacit agreement, they moved apart.

A curious, a close call: one either or both might have answered.

But all that occupied Sheldon now was the knowledge, the sensation, the reprieve from the dread that had gripped him during his illness and that had been born in Simona's bed yesterday afternoon:

Ah, but he was jubilant now. He would bless Marie forever. Including that stupid pile of books put there by some thoughtless workman.

After Marie left he picked up one of the books. The largest — it must have been the one that tripped Marie. It was one of those outsized volumes seen on coffee tables at Christmas time.

Except that this one happened to be more than

that: *The Connoisseur's Treasury of American Furniture,* authored by a museum curator, containing a preface by Sheldon Bradley. 1950.

Precisely at one o'clock he took the elevator up to Marie's apartment, arriving just after McFarland and the African Minister. And immediately the lanky arms trader was at the bar.

Drinks all around. Right?

"Marie—an aperitif? Cinzano or—"

"If you wouldn't mind, John, a little Scotch on the rocks, please."

"Scotch?" Surprised, McFarland chided her: "It'll be Alcoholics Anonymous for you next, sweetlove."

Marie's smile was constrained.

"Mr. Minister?"

"A sherry would be excellent, thank you." Kuandi seemed nervous as he seated himself on the sofa beside Marie. He was wearing a gray Savile Row suit which, in the clear October sunlight, had about it a kind of mothball vintage.

McFarland was saying: "Sheldon, are you still on those bloody fruit juices?"

"Yes. But for today how about a mild Bloody Mary?"

"I'll give it my best shot." McFarland turned to the cabinet, to the shelves with their formations of bottles like glass tenpins.

After his first sip of sherry, Kuandi rose and asked

if he might use the telephone. "I have been trying to contact my brother. I should like to ask the hotel operator to transfer the call to this number."

Marie showed him into an adjacent room.

Sheldon, standing at the bar next to McFarland, asked: "Is everything going all right, John? When I got here I thought you might have been a bit low?"

"Low? Preposterous." He went on, extravagantly: "Is the madam of a bustling brothel low on a Friday night when the moon is full and the air is a-cry with a hundred hot-peckered roosters?"

When Kuandi returned, his round, fleshy face was creased with concern: no, the operator had not yet been able to put the call through, no connection had been possible so far.

McFarland reminded him that Monaco was not famous for its telephone service. But somehow this did not seem to comfort the Minister.

And at the luncheon table Kuandi's taut, uncommunicative presence inspired long silences, and even the voluble McFarland was not up to his customary performance.

A mistake to have come. But McFarland had made the occasion sound as if it would be a virtual celebration of what was clearly the major weapons deal of his career. . . .

And now again the Defence Minister and McFarland were quietly discussing business: a vocabulary that was like a foreign tongue. He brought his attention back to Marie: how was her foot?

A slight swelling but she had soaked it in hot water and it was better now. She still seemed uneasy with him. Obviously she was aware of the particular exhilaration she'd brought him earlier.

Sheldon poured more wine into her glass.

"Marie, my sweetlove—" John McFarland's interruption.

"What?" She looked away from Sheldon, turning to her husband, but as she raised her hand she struck her wine glass and suddenly the white, lace-edged tablecloth was stained with the blood of claret. . . .

She buzzed for the maid, and McFarland said: "Spill your wine and you spill your secrets, my dad used to say."

"It—this must be one of those days." Marie's smile was too bright.

McFarland took a pinch of salt in his fingers and threw it over his left shoulder. To Kuandi: "Keeps away the demons. Do you have such a foolish superstition in your country, Mr. Minister?"

"We have our superstitions. But not this one." His attention drifted, and held then on the two pastel-blue telephones which stood on a small, veneered Louis XVI console table near the double-doored entry of the dining room. There were two telephones in every room. Except for John's private office, which had four.

Not long after lunch Kuandi announced that he would like to return to his hotel. Or perhaps try his luck at the Casino for a while. Obviously he was in need of distraction. Sheldon, too, had to leave. He'd call a taxi. The Minister, however, would be more than pleased to give him a lift in his car. And presently Sheldon was in the Westinghouse elevator, a stainless steel cubicle, with his unlikely companion, the Defence Minister in the gray, pin-striped uniform of the Western Establishment, which he would shed when he returned to his native land. Kuandi, stumpy and thickset, was already tugging on his pigskin gloves in youthful anticipation of being at the helm of the silver Porsche.

"You're sure this won't inconvenience you, Mr. Minister?"

"It will be my pleasure, Mr. Bradley."

18

It couldn't have been more than sixty seconds after McFarland's guests had gone that the telephone rang:

"Yes? Yes, Claude? He's here." Marie handed over the phone to him: her features were alive with alarm. Her brother, high in the echelons of police, only called or visited two or three times a year — on Marie's birthday in March or at Christmas or New Year's. . . .

But this was October.

"Hello, Claude — no, Kuandi is gone. Just left. Hotel or Casino. Oh, no! Almightygod no — Claude, everything I — no. I told you he left a minute ago — what? WHAT?"

Running, John hurled the news at Marie: the police were on their way to pick up Kuandi. To protect him. There had been a coup. Kuandi's government had been overthrown. His brother had been assassinated. . . .

Claude had warned that neither Marie nor John should leave the building.

But John was bounding out the door now and into the corridor, and he jabbed the button for the elevator. He waited there in his pulsating skin until, with maddeningly slow precision, the elevator door slid open.

Just as the descent began there was the terrible shattering roar that seemed to rise from the depths of the earth. A deafening thunder. Like a tank hitting a land mine—the explosive reverberations from below zoomed straight up the elevator shaft, the stainless steel cage shuddered:

John reached the subterranean level: the door of the elevator shaft into the garage had been blown off; his blood seemed to plummet from the back of his skull down to the small of his back:

Oh Godalmighty. He saw the Porsche. Or what was left of it. A black skeleton of a car. The concrete floor was a battlefield of plaster, steel, glass, chrome:

He saw a leg, pantless; on the foot was a brown suede shoe.

Terror clutched at him. Pandemonium. There was the janitor, the doorman. Police were arriving. People were running in down the long, curving ramp:

Twenty feet from the blown-up car lay Sheldon, his bloodied head unrecognizable:

Someone—the doorman—said he must have been struck by a flying fragment of steel, it must have killed him instantly. . . .

Jesus, Sheldon!

More police. No, nobody seemed to know what had happened, how it had happened. Everybody talking at once, a harsh cacophony of echoes in the garage.

Sirens now — the ambulance — the police cleared the area of people.

Claude now. The plain blue suit, holster beneath. But Claude hurried past him. "Marie—" her brother shouted, "get back upstairs—"

John turned, rushed toward Marie, told her what he knew. "Call Nick—tell him to call Simona! For christsakes, hurry, Marie—right away!" He pushed her, ashen and shaking, back into the elevator.

Then he confronted Claude: how could this have happened? How? He had to know. Now. But Claude only told him that yes, they had had Kuandi under surveillance but their man had left when he saw John and Kuandi coming into the Residence du Parc—at ten minutes to one — surely for lunch. But in the meanwhile there'd been the teletype flash. It would be broadcast on the next news program at four o'clock. . . .

The janitor now answered Claude's questions: he had seen a man—a white man—yes, a man he had never seen before—walking out of the garage just as he had returned from lunch. What time? About 1:30.

Yes, he would recognize him if he saw him, yes. No, no distinct features—but a white man.

"That's what we weren't looking for, John," Claude admitted. "A white man."

The ambulance was leaving, moving up the ramp: Sheldon's faceless corpse. And, oh Jesus, that leg of Kuandi's with that brown suede shoe. The rest of Kuandi—the pieces lumped in the cotton bag. . . . "Mr. Minister—" Oh Jesus Holy Mother Mary—my money, my check—oh Jesus. . . .

John turned and ran toward the elevator—and that eternal wait, all the way down now from that fucking thirtieth floor! Oh Holy Mother — hurry! Call the bank. Get hold of Willy. Jesus, where's that elevator.

Upstairs he ran to his office—shouting obscenities for all Monaco and the world to hear. That check better be — he telephoned the bank manager: "Mr. Boda—McFarland here. Has that check cleared? Has it gone through? Oh my god! When? Oh my God! No!"

"We just learned about it. That Swiss account has been blocked. We're sorry, sir—"

Sorry?

Every nickel he owned was riding on that check.

Think fast. Think, Johnnyboy. Get a hold of Willy. Now. Jesus this phone service here—! Get a hold of Kevin! Kevin — he would have to come up with a bundle. The IRS would never give him another week of grace. A straight million on that settlement. But they would never give him more grace.

"Willy—yes—yes—Willy, get a hold of our guys there. See if they can protect or reclaim at least the big stuff. No, goddamit, certainly not! You go ahead. Contact the rebel group. Get a hold of them! We'll ship them anything they want. Make it fast Willy! Today. Now. Call me. Willy—we're cleaned out— tell them I'll supply anything. But we have to have front money—tell 'em, and *Salem Maleikum* to the bloody bastards! Call me back!"

He hung up. He deactivated the scrambler.

Another phone was ringing.

Again, the bank manager, Mr. Boda: he had heard of the tragedy. What was to be done about the $500,000 loan from Mr. Bradley? His estate would demand accounting.

Mygod—bloodhound bastards wouldn't even give him time to breathe.

"Listen, Boda, give me some air! I'll get back to you tomorrow."

"Tomorrow." The banker repeated it and it ricocheted like mortar fire.

All this coming at him.

Jesus!

Sheldon. Dead. A corpse. Sheldon.

And that leg—the foot with that goddam shoe!

Oh, Holy Mother of God, what have they done to me!

As a boy he had been a supplicant before God. He grew up with faith. A believer. Until the world taught him otherwise.

"Always follow Christ, my son," his mother used to say.

Follow him where? To the poorhouse!

And now he was there. At the threshold.

Like Nick, like Sheldon, after all the smartass maneuvers to leave the States, to evade taxes, to shelter in Monaco, to live a protected life, he had ended up here: a haven turned to hell.

19

The crematorium was in Marseilles, about four hours from Monte Carlo; though for Nick driving Simona there in his battered TR 3 it seemed more like halfway around the world.

Far ahead and unseen, the hearse which had left earlier would be at the cemetery waiting for them.

Sometimes they talked, sometimes not. Simona in black slacks and black cardigan, her hair hooded by a violet scarf, sat too erectly in the bucket seat beside him, lighting one cigarette from another.

What ran through the reels of her mind? Had she, like Nick, been meditating on how unreal this drive was, this mission?

He and Simona, who had traveled to so many places, to so many terminals of gaiety — how could they now be en route to that ungayest of all terminals?

Sheldon: the peaceful, the elegant, always determined to protect himself from the imperfect, the ugly,
the violent. Sheldon, the least likely candidate. . . .

It had been a week since Nick had written to Marion.
Or had tried to. He'd try again tomorrow. Even
though he knew he'd tear it up. It had finally come
down to that. Her letters were less frequent now, her
pride had been bruised by his silences: but Nick
could no longer put his feelings on paper for his
letters always had to end in the same way: "Still no
visa, not yet."

He couldn't bring himself to give her false hopes.
Her commitment in New Mexico was as irrevocable
as his cancelled passport.

Simona's voice: "Would you mind stopping in
Cannes?"

He turned off the parkway at Antibes and took the
road along the sea; the sun was alternately shy and
bold. This was, after all, November third.

Into Cannes, along the Croisette which, as Sheldon
had often said, was "miraculous in an age of instant
tourism and highrise ghettos." For this was certainly
the most beautiful seafront boulevard; it had not lost
its glory. The low rooflines had been preserved.
Along this great sweeping curve with its two harbors,
the facades of its fin-de-siècle hotels, the flags and

flowers and palms, the shops and cafés—all of it had a cared-for look. And even now in November it somehow still presented a kind of summertime gaiety.

"Here Nick—can you stop here—the Blue Bar."

He parked in the no-parking zone and they went to a table on the sidewalk terrace.

Two coffees.

Simona's eyes showed a sudden lustre, or maybe it was the sudden sunlight. It was glittering off the sea and dappling the palm trees and playing on the flags flying from the Festival building next door. (Nick had once shown his bus passengers this scene during the annual Cannes Film Festival when the pavements and the Blue Bar were thick with all the bearded film freaks and hustlers and all the rich new directors and actors who looked so chic in their tattered poorboy clothes.)

"We came here. We had coffee here. Summer before last." Simona's voice was still faint, remote. "And Sheldon took me to see a tinsmith who worked in the Old Quarter. How he knew about him I never did learn. And then we climbed up to the church. And that view!" She turned and peered westward and beyond to the Esterel range rising in a blue mist out of the Mediterranean.

Another minute and the sun grew dim.

Abruptly Simona rose. Nick paid the check and they returned to the car. And he started back to the parkway. "Sorry," Simona was saying. "Sorry, Nick."

When he'd reached Simona's cottage that insane terrible afternoon earlier this week, he'd heard her
screams even before he'd entered. He'd found her in
the living room, beating the floor with her hands,
screaming: "No! No!—No, no!" The telephone was
beside her, the receiver off, the abrasive buzzing
beneath her sobs and moans and curses. He had
knelt beside her, had tried to talk to her, tried to hold
her. She would not listen. She refused to hear him.
He had poured some brandy and made her drink it,
had sat beside her on the floor, holding her, stroking
her back, her neck, holding her. For hours . . .

He knew she'd never get sleep without tranquiliz-
ers. And he knew there'd be none in her house. She
never used them. She did not believe in drugs. He'd
called his doctor to come. Her distended nerves
pleaded for sedation. But Simona in wild despair
had told the doctor: "No, no drugs! Please. I'm pregnant—"

Which was how Nick had learned:

Learned not only of her pregnancy but that she
evidently wanted to go through with it. There was no
mention of it again. Until last night:

And immediately he had perceived a puzzling new
texture in her voice: it wasn't elation, nor was it
alarm or fear; rather it had a certain meditative quality he had never observed in her before.

It had been one of her more rational intervals.
Though he still couldn't accustom himself to her talk
about a child. Their life together had been so free-

wheeling, aimless. In those days children were never in her consciousness. Or his . . . . With Jane it had been different. She had always wanted a child, she had talked about it with the same effusion she talked about her imaginary travel adventures. And when the doctor confirmed her pregnancy it had added another joyful dimension to their lives.

But Simona? Sheldon's child? A dead man's child?

Nick on that first night dared not leave her alone. He stayed with her and he slept next to her not even realizing until dawn that he was still in his clothes.

And he had had to make all the arrangements for Sheldon. Marie had offered to come and stay with Simona for the day, they couldn't leave her alone. Nick had picked up some clothes at his apartment and returned to Simona's to be with her while she had to wait for this last brutal ride.

It took four days before the cremation could be scheduled, before they could take Sheldon's body to the nearest crematorium, which was in Marseilles. And during that awful waiting, the only person who came to the house was Marie McFarland. She brought liquor and food. Her helpfulness seemed almost compulsive as if she knew of no other way to demonstrate her feelings over what had happened, as if she could mitigate her husband's unwitting connection with Sheldon's death.

Now, driving westward on the parkway, they were beyond the groves of umbrella pines and the turnoff for St. Tropez. Simona was very quiet again and there were more cigarettes. He had attempted to spare her this trip, he had offered to drive alone and . . .

"No," she'd insisted again that morning. "I want to be with him."

An hour and a half to go. She kept looking straight ahead.

After a while he tried again to talk about ordinary things. But he had exhausted small talk. And even big talk.

Then he told her that he would have to move. The owner was taking over his flat for his son and daughter-in-law. He had until January 1st. "And so here I am, Simona"—he kept his voice as light as he could—"a real estate maven like me, and I haven't come up with anything for myself."

She nodded, though she didn't seem to have heard him. "The cemetery—all of the—"

"I'm taking care of everything. Don't worry."

Yet a few minutes later Simona was saying, "You can always stay on the hill."

"What?"

"At my place. If you don't find anything."

"That's where I've been staying."

"Yes . . . ohgod, Nick—if you hadn't, what would I have done—?"

"Baby, forget it." He reached over and pressed her

hand. Her fingertips were cold. "You may not even be able to get rid of me."

When they neared Marseilles, Simona said: "I never cared one way or the other."

He looked at her.

"I mean about children."

"I know."

"God, Nick, it's all I have to hold on to, it's all I'll have left of—Did you send the telegram to his son? Oh yes, I asked you that before."

He had notified the son of the death and for him to contact Sheldon's lawyer in New York.

As for the apartment, she had asked Nick to put it up for sale. She would never be able to live there:

Live in that one condominium Sheldon had been obsessed to make his home:

How often, Nick kept thinking, how often he had tried to interest him in other buildings, other properties. But no way. It had to be the Residence du Parc.

In a patternless world there were these patterns. Just as in his own patternless life there had been the pattern that had led to Jane's murder: the one night he would be away from the apartment, that was the one time when he had agreed, after quitting the field, to do just one more TV commercial: they were shooting it at night, at one of those charity, fund-raising balls, and the champagne people wanted to use Nick. He had been job hunting, looking for something more productive, but it had been slow going and so he had promised to do the champagne segment:

With 365 nights in the year, why that one night, that one hour?

It was different with Kuandi. He was almost an inevitable victim of his time, his world.

Yet the greatest senselessness of all this was that John McFarland had escaped: the merchant of death was alive.

To Nick, fate, destiny, karma—these were abstractions. People got hung up on this, but he wasn't one of them. Or hadn't been. That had been more for Simona; she had often been on those metaphysical trips, including cosmobiology, but even Simona had kind of phased out. . . .

But now? Could he begin to accept a pattern?

Jane's death, Sheldon's death: they could almost have been charted on a graph. But he knew there was no place for graphs in a patternless world: you ended up realizing the unknown could never be known; that all there was was mystery.

And maybe that's all there was supposed to be.

The crematorium in the Marseilles cemetery was a low structure of neutral gray stone, the central section flanked by two curving wings faced with small square plaques behind which reposed the ashes of the dead. And Nick couldn't help grimly thinking it looked like a bank wall of marble safety deposit boxes.

The hearse was there waiting by the entrance.

Nick parked the TR 3, and Simona, wordless, left him to walk over to the hearse. She stood there as the two men, with the help of two more from the building, took the plain pine coffin out of the hearse and carried it inside on their shoulders.

The mourners' or visitors' hall was homogenized, non-denominational: benches on either side, and in the center of the rear wall a black curtain.

The coffin was set on a platform directly in front of the curtain. Again Simona left Nick and went over to the coffin. She touched it, her head lowered, her mouth and her eyes tightly shut as she invoked whatever meditation or prayer might have been left in her.

When she returned to sit beside Nick on the bench, one of the men raised the black curtain and then the coffin was pushed through into darkness:

Nick felt the current in her body, the sudden stiffening. He grasped her elbow as they rose to leave. And then came, from behind the curtained wall, that dreadful and arresting sound.

Simona halted, turned to him: What was that?

"Nothing." But Nick had recognized it, yes, that same sound he'd heard in the crematorium back home when he had gone through all this after Jane's death: it was the clang of the iron door after the coffin had been consigned to the furnace:

And now once again:

Simona was still looking back to where the sound had come: she must have known, for her body quivered and he saw her swallow.

"Let's go." He gripped her, his voice was harsh, he had to break the constriction in his throat.

Approaching them was a man from the crematorium. Nick should have remembered. Yes. The man wished to know what type of urn or container was preferred.

Nick consulted Simona. No response, her lips were colorless, blanched. "Simona — they have to know. For the ashes. An urn or what do you—"

"Don't know—"

"Simona—"

The man in his black suit, white shirt, black tie waited patiently, that look on his drooping face: Condolences Anonymous.

"Simona—"

"It doesn't matter, does it matter?" And then: "I don't know. Don't care—anything—a goddamn Dixie cup—!"

POST-MORTEM

That Monte Carlo season had passed, and for my friends a period of trial and tragedy had ended. But for me, the end, as such, loomed with an added and curious poignancy the following year, during the early summer of 1976.

It was not much different from other seasons. But I was fascinated seeing it come to life: I have always found a special or private pleasure in witnessing the transition of resorts from winter or spring into summer:

Facades of cafés and restaurants were being freshly painted, new awnings replaced the ones that had become frayed or sun-faded. The verdant park sloping down toward the cream-colored Casino was bordered by a profusion of brilliant young blooms and the leaves of the great magnolia trees shone with a new patina. And the waiters of the Café de Paris seemed to have shed the winter skins of their lethargy, and the croupiers arriving at the Casino for the day's or the night's work stepped with a livelier pace; and the yachts, out of drydock, scraped and painted, flaunted their sleek new whiteness in the blue harbor.

Past, and remembered, was the Monte Carlo Grand Prix, the shattering roar of those racing cars still reverberating in my ears.

The barroom of the Hotel de Paris once again began to fill with the familiar faces of the ever familiar international rich—all those regulars who glided through life as if chaos, anarchy and terror didn't exist in the world, as if the world was nothing more than a series of drawing rooms or gilded enclaves in which they met in their eternal battle against boredom.

From time to time I saw Marie and John McFarland, and he still showed that same wild Irish rose of a face. He had managed to survive the debacle of the previous summer: less than a week after the death of Sheldon and the Defence Minister, he flew to Africa and went directly to Kuandi's country where he set up a new agreement to supply an arsenal of weapons for the rebels who had seized power. He made me realize how true that cynical axiom of the arms traders was: "No matter who wins, we win; no matter who loses, we win."

And I remember how Sheldon had once quipped

to him: "My mistake, John, is that I've spent my life concentrating on legs instead of aı ns."

What I didn't realize until after Sheldon's death was that despite his unobtrusive ways he had really been the pivotal force of that group, and his name kept coming up so often, his presence so pervasive that it almost seemed, at times, as if he were still living.

I saw Nick frequently; he was still in real estate, though he was now working more out of an office than out of the bar of the Hotel de Paris. . . .

The recollection that lingers most vividly is that morning in June when I met Nick and Simona at the arcaded outdoor market, busily domestic, loading their basket of vegetables and fruit into the old TR 3. As for Simona, her memorably svelte body was now expanded into the formidable and, for her, somehow unlikely bulge of advanced pregnancy. Of course she was not quite the same spirited and exuberant Simona I'd come to know. She was more muted, her face a bit drawn and somber. Her eyes, however, conveyed a kind of serene resignation.

And, oh yes, there was one more encounter, or event, that belongs in this record: it took place on the night of July 4th at the Summer Sporting Club. It was a gala, and very dressy indeed, and attended by what looked like every American resident or visitor on the entire Riviera. For this was the occasion celebrating the Bicentennial of the United States:

The entrance hall was festive with garlands of flowers and swags of bunting; and on the main wall, a photo mural of George Washington and one of Gerald Ford. On one side of the great hall, hanging from a lofty, gold-tipped staff, was the red and white flag of Monaco; on the opposite side hung the Stars and Stripes; and standing there, beneath it, was a member of the local welcoming committee. I looked at him twice to make sure; then I was sure: it was none other than my fair-haired friend, one true-blue Harper Nicholson.